I0685609

A HEART REDIRECTED

PEACOCK HILL ROMANCE BOOK 4

ELIZABETH MADDREY

Copyright © 2019 by Elizabeth Maddrey

All rights reserved.

No part of this book may be reproduced in any form or by any electronic or mechanical means, including information storage and retrieval systems, without written permission from the author, except for the use of brief quotations in a book review.

Scripture quoted by permission. Quotations designated (NIV) are from THE HOLY BIBLE: NEW INTERNATIONAL VERSION®. NIV®. Copyright © 1973, 1978, 1984 by Biblica. All rights reserved worldwide.

Cover design by Jennifer Zemanek of Seedlings Design Studio

Published in the United States of America by Elizabeth Maddrey - www.ElizabethMaddrey.com

Publisher's Note: This novel is a work of fiction. Names, characters, places, and incidents are either products of the author's imagination or used fictitiously. All characters are fictional, and any similarity to people living or dead is purely coincidental.

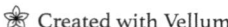 Created with Vellum

For everyone who struggles to release control and let Jesus make His plan for their life known.

In their hearts humans plan their course,
but the Lord establishes their steps.

— PROVERBS 16:9

1

Cheerful yellow and white daffodils speared out of the urns spaced down both sides of Peacock Hill's chapel garden. The beds were a riot of color from more daffodils, crocuses, and hyacinths—all the early April blooms. White chairs sat in even rows facing the little raised gazebo at the front of the space, and guests chatted quietly with one another as a string quartet played in the background.

Sean Fitzgerald checked his watch again and frowned.

Larissa—the bride—was ready. She and her attendants were all waiting in one of the sunken gardens at the side of the mansion. This wasn't the first wedding at Peacock Hill, but it was the first since the property had been available as an official wedding venue. Sean had become friends with Deidre McIntyre —well, Crawford now—over the last eight months. This wedding was as important to her as it was to the bride and groom. Which begged the question: where was the groom?

Sean strode through the hedge-framed archway and out onto the large lawn. He crossed to where the best man and groomsmen stood huddled in a circle.

"Any luck?"

The best man shook his head. "He's not answering."

Sean's stomach twisted. Now what? "Okay. Who has a car?"

One of the groomsmen raised his hand.

"Great. Drive to the hotel and find him."

The man's eyes bugged. "It's twenty minutes away."

"Do you have a better idea?" Sean glanced at his watch again. Twenty minutes there. The groom had better be dressed and ready to go. Twenty minutes back. What was he supposed to tell everyone to explain a forty-minute delay? His phone rang and he blew out a breath and answered. "Where are you?"

"I can't do it."

Sean took a few steps away from the huddle of groomsmen. "What? I know I didn't hear that right."

"I can't. Larissa's a great girl—woman—whatever, but I can't marry her."

"Just wait one sec—"

"Tell her I'm sorry, okay?"

The line went dead. Sean closed his eyes. In all his years as a wedding planner, this had never happened. Now what?

The best man tapped him on the shoulder. "Was that him?"

"Yeah."

"He's not coming, is he?"

Sean frowned at the man. "You knew."

He shook his head. "Suspected. Hoped I was wrong. You want me to tell Larissa?"

"No. It's okay. I can do it. Just hang here with the rest of the guys, and don't say anything to anyone yet." Stomach in his shoes, Sean slipped back into the hedge-lined garden and approached the bride's parents. He stooped and lowered his voice. "Mr. and Mrs. Carey, could you come with me, please?"

Mrs. Carey frowned and glanced at her husband.

Mr. Carey's face flushed with anger as he stood.

Sean fought a wince. Looked like Larissa's dad knew what

was happening. Sean jerked his head toward the nearest arch leading out of the garden. The couple followed him.

A hand landed on his shoulder like lead. Sean turned and met Mr. Carey's eyes.

"He's not coming, is he? That—"

"Honey." Mrs. Carey slipped her hand through her husband's elbow. "Larissa needs us."

"Never liked that boy. You know that."

"I do. So does Larissa. So, probably, does Tom."

Mr. Carey grunted and turned back to Sean. "Have you told her yet?"

"Not yet. I thought maybe you'd want to be nearby."

"That's thoughtful." Mrs. Carey patted her husband's arm. "Come on, honey. Let's go to our girl."

Sean swallowed and headed toward the sunken garden where the ladies were waiting. How was he supposed to do this? Did he tell her fast, like ripping off a bandage? Or was it better to ease into it?

The women all turned his way when he started down the marble steps. Larissa looked radiant in her princess-style gown. Layers of tulle fluffed around her waist and fell to the ground, offsetting the sleek lines of the fitted bodice. She'd had cap sleeves added for modesty, and the effect was stunning.

And now he had to break her heart.

Sean cleared his throat. "Ladies. Could I speak to you a moment, Larissa?"

"Of course." She lifted her skirt and crossed to him, confusion working across her features as she spotted her parents. "What's wrong? Where's Tom?"

Like a bandage, then. "He's not coming."

Shock and disbelief flitted across her features as her eyes filled. She looked over Sean's shoulder, blinking. "Mom?"

Her mother hurried down the stairs, her arms open. "Oh, baby, I'm sorry."

Larissa flung herself into her mother's embrace.

"That boy better hope I never come across him in a dark alley," Mr. Carey muttered as he passed Sean and folded his wife and daughter into his embrace.

Sean stood for a moment, watching. There were details that needed to be taken care of. It was still his job to do that, even if there wasn't going to be a wedding. He took a deep breath. "I can only imagine how hard this is, but I need to know how you'd like me to handle your guests. I'm sorry."

Larissa drew in a sharp breath and straightened. She wiped her eyes and nodded. "Of course. The guests. We have all this food—the cake, the s'mores? We might as well have a party. It can be my near-miss celebration."

"Larissa." Her mother's voice held censure and a tiny undercurrent of amusement.

"Mom, come on, if he's willing to leave me at the altar, was he going to stay when things got hard? I guess I didn't know him as well as I thought I did." She managed a watery laugh. "It just goes to prove that long engagements don't guarantee anything."

"You're amazing." The words slipped out before Sean could stop them. It wasn't that they weren't true. Nothing could be truer. But if there was one generally agreed rule in the wedding planning industry, it was not to fall in love with the bride. And if that first rule got broken? It was probably smarter not to let on.

"WELL, THAT COULD HAVE GONE BETTER." Sean collapsed onto a couch in the room Deidre Crawford, the owner of Peacock Hill, had designated a TV or hangout room for eventual guests when they opened as a retreat center. He glanced at Anna Hamilton—

soon to be McIntyre—and grimaced. "Still, your s'mores were a hit."

"Those were more Azure's doing than mine, but yeah. Even if it was weird to go ahead with the party when the wedding didn't happen. I'm not sure I'd have the grace Larissa showed."

"Yeah?" Duncan, Anna's fiancé, took her hand. "What would you do instead?"

"Get in a car and hunt you down. So don't get any ideas, buster."

Sean laughed. "I'd believe her if I were you, Duncan."

"I do. But hey, look at that, I've already got my lines down, so there's nothing to worry about."

Sean fought the surge of jealousy that reared up at Duncan's teasing words. Not that he was carrying any sort of torch for Anna. The brief time they'd dated had convinced him they were better as friends. Much better. And Duncan? He was perfect for Anna. They were almost too cute for words a lot of the time. He cleared his throat. "Any progress on a wedding date you two?"

"Don't start. Please." Duncan held up his hands. "We're getting enough of that from everyone else. The gardens need a lot of attention right now. It's spring."

"I still think we should elope. You know I don't want a big fuss. We could go over to Charlottesville and get it done, come home, and take up residence in our cottage. Together." Anna cast an imploring glance in Sean's direction. "Can't you convince him that's reasonable?"

"Don't look at me. I'm a wedding planner, remember? I love the big fuss." He studied the couple for a moment before shrugging. "That said, she has a point. If the gardens are really going to keep you from having a wedding this spring—which I'm not sure I understand, mind you, but whatever—then what are we looking at? Labor Day?"

"We had projects booked all fall last year. That's hopefully going to be the case again this year. At least, if we want the business to keep solvent. If you're going to insist we can't get married until work has slowed down, it'll be November at least." Anna shrugged.

Duncan frowned.

Anna pointed at him. "You know I'm right."

"Maybe, but I don't want to get married at the courthouse. What if we did something small, like Deidre did last Christmas? Then at least our parents could come. Friends." Duncan glanced over at Sean. "How hard is it to pull something like that together?"

"It depends." There were things like flowers and food to consider. A pastor. Invitations? Or would they just call people up and give them the information. "You'd still need a date."

Duncan looked at Anna and bit his lower lip. "Two weeks?"

Anna squealed. "Really?"

"If Sean says it's possible."

Two sets of eyes zeroed in on him. Sean swallowed and dug his phone out of his pocket. He brought up his schedule and puffed out his cheeks. "I can't do a weekend. My weekends are spoken for through mid-July."

"Wednesday? Thursday? Tuesday? I'm not picky, are you?" Anna looked at Duncan. He shook his head.

"How about the twenty-third? It's a Tuesday and it's just over two weeks away, which buys us a tiny bit of extra time." Sean tapped the square on his calendar to expand it to the day view. It was blank. That was a minor miracle in and of itself. "But when you say simple, you need to mean it."

"I do." Anna grinned. "I'm good with that if you are, Duncan."

"You're sure?" Duncan gazed at Anna. Then, as if he saw whatever it was he was looking for, he nodded. "All right. Let's do this."

Anna leaned over and kissed Duncan.

Sean looked away. He wasn't jealous. Maybe only in the abstract sense. He blocked off the date on his phone then cleared his throat. "I'd been planning to head back to Richmond in the morning, but if the two of you are free, it'd be good to spend time going over details. Even simple, there's a lot of work to do between now and the twenty-third."

"After church? We could grab some takeout for lunch on the way home and then spend as much of the afternoon as you can spare." Anna glanced at Duncan for confirmation before returning her gaze to Sean.

Right. Church. That wouldn't have slipped his mind if he'd been in Richmond, but something about the disconnectedness of Peacock Hill had sent it flying away. "Sure. If I leave here by five I'll get home in enough time to do a quick check of everything I need to get ready for Monday."

"Five hours should be more than enough." Duncan's laugh hitched as Sean shook his head. "Seriously? What are we possibly going to talk about for five hours? It's a wedding, not a major military invasion."

"A wedding that we're putting together in under three weeks. And we don't have the resources of the U.S. Army behind us. So those five hours? They're not going to be the end of talking to me."

"Did you forget simple? We're going for simple." Duncan's voice had a panicked edge that, under different circumstances, would have made Sean chuckle.

"Sometimes simple can be harder. Let's see how we do tomorrow, and we'll go from there. All right?" Sean stood. "I put my stuff up on the third floor—Deidre said it was fine—so I'm going to turn in."

Anna grinned and hopped off the arm of the couch to give

him a quick hug. "Thanks, Sean. I know this is a wrench in your plans."

"Anything for a friend." He patted her shoulder and nodded at Duncan. "Night, man."

As he climbed the fantastic staircase that was the centerpiece of Peacock Hill's main floor, indistinct murmurs reached his ears. Sean pictured Duncan and Anna wound around one another saying good night as only a couple deliriously in love could do.

He sighed and closed his eyes. As much as it had been torture to help Larissa plan her wedding, seeing her devastated when Tom didn't show had broken his heart. She deserved so much more. Larissa had disappeared before the reception was over and he hadn't been able to track her down. Hopefully one of her bridesmaids or her parents had taken her home and was staying with her. She shouldn't be alone.

Sean pushed away the longing to be the one to comfort her and tell her this was for the best. It wasn't his place.

It never would be.

2

L arissa Carey stared at her reflection. She wouldn't be winning any beauty awards today. Dark circles sagged under her bloodshot eyes like bruises. Her skin was paler than if she was emerging from a month-long sickness. She scooped her hair into a knot at the base of her skull and turned from the mirror. It didn't matter what she looked like, not when she was staring down the prospect of returning to Richmond alone, when she should be heading for the airport with her new husband, to board a flight to the Miami and the cruise terminal.

She pressed her fingers to her lips and drew in a long shaky breath through her nose. Her stomach twisted.

Tom.

Larissa blinked back the tears that threatened. She was done wasting time on him. What kind of man walked away from the woman he'd asked to marry him when she was standing in her gown, waiting? And why hadn't he come and talked to *her*? Called *her*?

He'd called Sean.

Heat washed over her face. Sean had been so kind. So obviously nervous about breaking the news. So heartbroken for her.

Larissa blew out her breath and tossed the last of her things into her carry-on bag and zipped it closed. At least she'd had the sense to send her dress and the larger suitcase home with her parents.

With the bag rolling behind her, Larissa slipped out of the guest room at Peacock Hill and down the hall to the grand staircase. She paused on the enormous landing, her eyes roving over the stained glass window that featured peacocks strutting on a mountainside, a glimpse of this mansion on one corner. It was a masterpiece, especially in the pale early morning light. She wasn't likely to see it again—as much as she loved Peacock Hill, there were memories here that were best forgotten. She tugged her phone out of the pocket of the purse dangling off her shoulder and snapped a photo before grabbing the handle of her suitcase and starting down the steps.

The scent of bacon drifted through the main foyer. Larissa's stomach gurgled in response. Maybe whoever was cooking had a spare slice. She hadn't been able to force down anything at the near-miss party that should've been her reception. All that food. She'd been so excited about those plans—Tom was supposed to have been amazed. He didn't even bother to show up to see the effort she'd put into starting their life together.

Enough. No more Tom. Bacon, then home.

She left her suitcase and purse against the wall near the door and followed her memory to the door she thought led to the kitchen. After a light tap, she pushed it open, her lips curving a smidgen when she saw the retro counter and appliances. Sean watched a pan at the stove, a 1950's era apron—ruffles and all—tied around his neck and waist.

He glanced up and frowned. "What are you doing here?"

She jolted back and her jaw dropped open. "I—sorry. I'll go."

"No. That came out wrong." Sean dropped his spatula on the counter and crossed the room in three long strides. He reached for her, his fingertips brushing against her arm, before he drew back and tucked his hands into his pockets. "I thought you'd left. Yesterday. After—I looked for you during the gathering."

Ah. She gave a tiny shrug. "I couldn't stay, but I didn't want to go back home with my parents. They kept talking about Tom, and I just—"

Sean nodded. "Want some bacon?"

"I really do."

He chuckled. "You're in luck. It happens I made extra. I can throw together some eggs, too, if you want?"

"Only if you're making some for yourself." Eggs weren't her thing, but she could choke them down if she needed to. She'd certainly done it enough times for Tom. She sighed.

"What?" Sean pointed to the kitchen table. "Why don't you take a seat? It's nearly ready."

Larissa pulled out a chair and sat. She ought to offer to help. She could get plates or napkins. Drinks. But she couldn't quite get herself moving.

Sean carried a plate piled with bacon and set it in the center of the table, then slid an empty plate in front of Larissa. "Dig in. Want some coffee?"

"I can get it."

"It's no problem. I need to get mine. Cream and two sugars, right?"

She nodded. Why did Sean remember that when Tom never did? She'd been dating Tom for four years. They'd been engaged for one and a half of those years. Even though—despite Tom's insistence that she was old fashioned and ridiculous—they'd never lived together, they'd met for breakfast or coffee. He should have picked up on her preferences. If he'd been paying attention. Clearly he hadn't been.

Sean set the mug of perfectly tan liquid in front of her. The scent combined with the bacon to make an aroma that had to be what wafted down the streets of heaven.

"Thanks."

Sean glanced up from loading bacon onto his own plate, and his gaze locked with hers. "My pleasure. How are you?"

Larissa shook her head and reached for a strip of bacon. "I don't even know how to answer that. I'll be okay, but I'm not. Not yet."

"Sure. Of course." He frowned and stared at his plate before looking back across the table at her. "How can I help?"

Larissa took a drink of coffee. There were things that had to be undone. A lot of them. She'd planned to spend her afternoon making lists and working up the nerve to get started making calls. None of that was Sean's responsibility. Or even his concern. He was her wedding planner. And maybe a friend. They'd certainly spent enough time together over the last fourteen months to qualify as something more than acquaintances, but this was over and above. "You don't happen to know an event unplanner, do you?"

He chuckled. "Would you believe that's not a high-demand career?"

She smiled.

"That said, I can help you make calls. The event stuff—I've got that covered already—but if you want help returning gifts and that kind of thing? I'm your man."

"At least I have one who's willing to stick around." Larissa's hand flew to her mouth. "I'm sorry. I—you're not—I shouldn't—"

"Relax." Sean laughed and reached for another slice of bacon. "I'm going to church with the gang here in about an hour. After that, I need to spend some of the afternoon with Duncan and Anna getting things organized for their . . . event."

"You can say wedding. I'm not that fragile." But it was nice that he cared enough to try to tiptoe. That kind of concern was typical for Sean, and completely the opposite of anything Tom would've done. Tom was a big fan of the school of suck it up. Well, in the end, what he'd taught her would help her get over him. So the joke, if there was one, was on Tom.

"Right. They decided they want to get it done in two weeks."

Larissa snickered. "Sure they did. I don't know either of them well, but from seeing them when we've come down here to plan? They're not the spontaneous types. Next April even seems a little fast for them. When's the wedding, for real?"

"Fifteen days."

"You're serious?"

Sean nodded.

"Wow. Maybe you should arrange for all your hesitant clients to attend a jilting."

Sean winced. "I don't—"

"It's fine. I said it, not you. There's no pretty word for what happened. Which is good, because it wasn't pretty. I got jilted, plain and simple. The sooner I figure out how to live with that, the better off everyone's going to be." Larissa drained her coffee and glanced across the kitchen. There was still more in the pot. She rose and crossed to the carafe. "So you have wedding talk with Anna and Duncan, then you're heading back to Richmond?"

"Yeah. We could get together this evening. Maybe for dinner? Start putting lists together?"

"Sure. Thank you." Larissa carried her coffee back to the table. "I can start working on the lists when I get home, to save you some time."

"If you want. Don't push yourself too hard, okay? You need time to grieve. And heal."

Larissa forced her lips into a smile. Pushing herself was the only thing that would keep her moving forward, and forward was the direction she had to go. Grieving? Healing? Those didn't need to factor in. At all. She'd simply put this behind her, adjust, and keep marching, because she'd fall apart if she stopped for too long. And there was nobody around who was going to help her pick up the pieces.

LARISSA PLOPPED on the bottom stair in front of Peacock Hill and sighed. She had no car. Of course she had no car. She'd driven down with her maid of honor and had planned to leave with her husband. That had slipped her mind when she'd sent her parents off last night. They had an early flight this morning. The last thing they needed to do was disrupt their lives even more simply because their daughter had chosen a louse for a fiancé.

At least she hadn't married him.

She reached for her phone. A taxi would cost the world, but maybe a nearby rental car company could bring her wheels.

"Hey." Sean paused on the last step. "I figured you'd be long gone by now."

"Yeah, me too. No car."

"No . . . right. I can take you home."

She shook her head. "I've disrupted enough of your weekend already, I couldn't ask—"

"You didn't. I offered."

"I really don't want to be a burden." That wasn't something she'd ever wanted to be. It was bad enough her parents were going to be saddled with bills for a wedding that never happened. She'd figure out a way to pay them back.

"It's not a problem. I live in Richmond too, remember?" His grin faltered. "Let me see if I can get Duncan before church starts. I'll need to reschedule the meeting to a phone conference this afternoon."

"Sean, really. Thanks, but don't. That's a lot of trouble. I was just going to look for a rental car."

"Closest one is Waynesboro. That's almost an hour. And that's only if they have cars and can get one out here today. This isn't a big deal. I'm sure Duncan will understand."

Larissa opened her mouth to object, but Sean turned away. After a moment, he held his phone to his ear. She crossed her arms. Stubborn man. She hadn't seen this side of him when he was planning all the wedding details. Oh, sure, he had ideas and suggestions when she was drawing a blank, but he was always deferential to her wishes. Must be the difference between how he treated clients and friends.

Sean faced her again, phone still to his ear. "Perfect. Thanks, man. Yep. Okay, later." He ended the call and nodded. "See? All set. Give me just a couple of minutes to grab my bags and we'll hit the road."

"You were going to church."

He shrugged. "I'll stream the service from home later. This is fine. Unless you don't want to ride with me? I'm kind of a reminder of the whole debacle yesterday. I should've thought of that. I'll call someone else. I bet Azure would take you, if you don't mind waiting until after church. She loves to drive. Her truck isn't the most comfortable, but it'll get you there."

"It's fine. This is fine." Larissa blinked as her eyes filled. "I don't want to be a bother. Go get your bags. I'll wait."

Sean bit his lip. He looked like he wanted to say something. If he asked her if she was okay, she was going to lose the slim hold she had on her emotions. She wasn't okay, and despite what she'd been telling everyone who asked, she didn't believe she ever would be again.

"I'll be quick."

She watched him take the steps two at a time then turned and looked out over the lawn stretching in front of the mansion.

A tear slipped down her cheek. Then another. Larissa pressed the heels of her hands to her eyes. She was not going to cry. Not now. Not ever, if she could help it. She took a deep, shuddering breath and held it. She counted to seven before slowly letting it out. Steadier, she opened the camera on her phone and zoomed in on spring sun filtering through leaves to create a dappled pattern on the ground. She took the photo, zoomed out and framed another shot of the gorgeous grounds.

They'd sent the wedding photographer home as soon as they'd realized Tom wasn't coming. It wasn't like Larissa wanted photos of the "Hey, we have all this food here that we paid for, so we might as well eat" party. Or the pictures taken prior to the ceremony—her mother helping her dress, a quiet moment with her dad—they should have been special memories, but what came after was going to cloud them for a long time. She didn't need photographic evidence of just how unlovable she was.

"Ready?" Sean jogged down the steps, carrying a hanging bag, with an overstuffed backpack slung over one shoulder.

"Yeah." She stood and dusted off her jeans before reaching for her suitcase. "I appreciate this. Will you add gas and mileage to my final bill?"

Sean stopped and frowned at her.

Larissa fought the urge to squirm. "What? It's the least I can do."

"I'm going to give you a little extra leeway because I know you're hurting. I can only imagine what you're going through. But hear me when I tell you I won't be doing that, and it's about all I can manage not to be insulted you think I would."

"But—"

He held up a hand. "Stop while you're behind."

Was it so wrong to offer to compensate him for taking her back to Richmond? He'd had to rearrange plans and leave earlier than he wanted. His afternoon conference was going to be done remotely instead of in person—and having tried to do several online consultations with Tom at the beginning of their planning, she knew that was less than optimal.

Larissa reached for the handle of her suitcase again and jolted when her fingers brushed his. "I can get it."

"So can I." He held her gaze until she sighed and looked away. "Go get in the car, Larissa."

Whatever. If he needed to be some kind of stubborn knight in shining armor, so be it. Right now, the only thing she cared about was that he had a steed—in this case, a sedan—that would get her home.

3

Sean got them headed down the windy road leading to the highway. Larissa stared out the passenger window. Was she angry at him or just angry in general? Not that she didn't have ample reason to be upset. Tom was an idiot.

"I couldn't agree more."

Sean glanced over. "Huh?"

"Tom's an idiot. Although I've been using stronger words in my head. I'm trying to back away from them. Too much swearing, even in my mind, and I get caught up in it. I had a horrible mouth in high school. It took a lot to stop."

"Never would have imagined that. Not ever."

Larissa shrugged. "Comes from the crowd you hang with, to some degree."

It probably did. "I mostly hung out with my youth group from church."

"Me too." She sighed. "Freshman year, the youth pastor talked about how doing something in your head was the same to God as doing it for real—you know the whole Sermon on the Mount thing where Jesus says if you look at someone lustfully it's the same as committing adultery?"

"Sure. We need to guard our thoughts."

She nodded. "Right. Well, everyone got on this kick about how if thinking the swear words was sin, we might as well go ahead and say them out loud. Keeping quiet didn't change anything."

"I'm not sure that's what Jesus was trying to say." Sean signaled and changed lanes to go around the eighteen-wheeler lumbering down the highway. "What made you decide to quit?"

"One, my parents agreed with you that it wasn't what God meant. But mostly? Letting those words have free reign in my head started me justifying letting other stuff have free reign there. Things I knew were wrong, but it wasn't as easy to turn my back on them. For me, swearing was kind of the gateway drug. And it's still a temptation."

"Huh. But idiot is okay?"

She laughed. "If we're back to talking about Tom, yes."

"Has he contacted you at all? Offered an explanation?" The guy hadn't been very forthcoming when he'd called Sean. Not that it was Sean's business, but Larissa deserved to know what was going on.

"Not that I know of, but I've been ignoring my phone. I've got a ton of notifications—email, Facebook, Instagram—and I can't bring myself to look. If I could, I'd pack everything up and disappear. Start a new life somewhere nobody knows I'm the girl who got left at the altar."

"Why can't you?" It wasn't what he wanted by a long shot, but he understood the desire. He'd been tempted to run a number of times in his life, but there'd always been some sort of tie holding him in place. "Your job, sure, but can't you do that anywhere?"

"If there's Internet, yeah." She sighed. "Of course, most of my students knew I was supposed to be getting married and on my honeymoon for the next two weeks. So it's not like I can completely escape. Even if I run, I'll need to support myself, and that means continuing to work with students who know all about the wedding that never was."

What was the right response? Was there one? "Mmm."

She chuckled. "Anyway, you can't run from your problems, can you? Not really. At some point you always end up having to face them."

"True." Sean glanced over and his heart broke. She looked defeated. Resigned. "You know it's going to be okay eventually, right?"

"Is it?"

"Well, I can't promise, obviously, but if I were a betting man, I'd take the odds. Maybe you'll even decide this was a good thing." Hadn't she said something along those lines at the time?

"Oh, it is. Sort of. I mean, if Tom wasn't sure about the marriage, I'd just as soon he figured that out ahead of saying 'I do.' But how do I trust myself again? The fact is I invested a lot of years into my relationship with him. I was ready to pledge the rest of my life to him. And still, he walked away whistling, while I stood in a white gown, waiting."

"I'm not positive he was whistling."

Larissa shook her head. "You know what I mean. Were there signs I missed? Shouldn't I have known—or at least suspected— this was coming?"

There'd been signs. Little ones, at least. Sean had even had two different conversations with Tom about his lack of involvement in the wedding planning. The man had played them off, said the wedding was for the woman and the marriage for the man. Like Sean hadn't heard that wheeze from other grooms who didn't want to be bothered with making the day special for their bride. The track record of those marriages wasn't stellar. Sean had wrestled with telling Larissa his concerns, but ultimately decided it wasn't his place. He was just the wedding planner.

"No comment?" She shifted in her seat and frowned at him. "When I said that to my parents and my bridesmaids, they assured me there was nothing to see."

Sean cleared his throat and stared at the road ahead. If it wouldn't be too obvious, he'd reach for the radio and turn it on. Or ask if she wanted to listen to music. Anything to change the subject.

"What do you know?"

"I don't *know* anything. Other than what Tom said when he called on Saturday, which was basically nothing."

"But you saw signs?"

Trapped, Sean lifted a shoulder. "I don't know if I'd call them signs. I had concerns. I addressed them with Tom, he assured me they were unfounded, and I moved on."

"But you didn't mention them to me."

It wasn't a question. He could have defended himself against a question. Or tried to, at least. Her quiet statement, filled with resignation and sorrow, tore at him. "What if I'd been wrong? How could I live with myself if I brought something up—an issue Tom himself dismissed—and it caused a fight between the two of you? What if saying something caused you to break your engagement when staying silent wouldn't have? I did the best I could with the information I had."

"In this case, you know you should have done more."

"Hindsight. In hindsight, yes, I wish I'd said something." Sean turned and met her accusing gaze, his heart sinking into his stomach. It wasn't as if he expected her to throw herself into his arms, but they'd had a friendship and, in time, maybe it could have turned into something. That seemed unlikely now. "You have no idea how much I regret that I didn't."

"Yeah? Me, too." Larissa buried her face in her hands and

took a deep breath. "Maybe you should put on some music. I don't think I want to talk to you anymore."

Her words sent a spear of pain lancing through him. She was entitled to feel that way. To blame him. It wasn't his fault—it was Tom's—but Sean would shoulder some of the hurt if it helped Larissa. Nodding, he pushed the button to turn on the radio.

"DID YOU HAVE A GOOD DRIVE HOME?" Anna leaned forward so her head blocked Duncan's in the window of Sean's laptop.

What was she digging for? Had he been too obvious about his interest in Larissa and someone noticed? Wouldn't that just be grand? "Sure. No traffic, no speed traps. Sorry we have to do this online. It's a little trickier."

"Pfft." Anna leaned back and rested her head on Duncan's shoulder. "We're just glad to get things rolling. Right, Duncan?"

"Right." He flashed a grin. "You're sure I need to be here?"

"I am." Anna's elbow jabbed backward into Duncan's ribs. "Can it, buster. What's first?"

Sean pushed lingering thoughts of Larissa's stony silence from his mind and focused on his calendar. "You cleared the date with Deidre?"

Duncan nodded. "She said even if there'd been a reservation she would've kicked them out."

"I'll keep that in mind if anyone else down there decides to set a speedy wedding date." Sean shook his head. "She knows that's bad business, right?"

"She was joking. Mostly. But I am her brother. That has to come with some perks, doesn't it?"

He'd drop everything if one of his siblings needed his help, so it made sense. But that didn't mean it wasn't also bad business. "I guess. Moot point, right? Venue's locked. You said simple, and we have to stick to that because of the time frame, but how casual do you want it to be? There's room for formal even if we're going simple."

Anna's eyes lit.

Sean smiled to himself and made a check beside formal on his list. Women could protest all they wanted about not needing all the fancy trappings on their wedding day, but he'd never met a bride who meant it deep down. The key—simple and rushed or elaborate with tons of planning time—was to narrow down the pieces that mattered and find a way to deliver them. He was good at it. It's what got him referrals.

He wouldn't be getting one from Larissa.

He spent almost three hours on the teleconference with Duncan and Anna. Anna had solid ideas which should be doable in the time. That was positive. Even better, Duncan hadn't been shy about expressing his opinions. And he'd had some. Unlike Tom.

How had Larissa not noticed her fiancé never had an opinion about wedding details? Or that he was never able to attend venue tours, vendor interviews, or even the cake tastings? Most men would show up to try food, at a minimum. Not Tom. Larissa always brushed off his absence. He was busy and important and blah blah blah. If Sean ever reached a point that he was too busy to plan the rest of his life with the woman he loved, someone needed to go ahead and shoot him.

Not that he was likely to get a chance with the woman he loved. Larissa had been colder than ice for the remainder of their drive home. She'd barely said anything—just the absolute minimum to let him know she wouldn't need his help untangling the mess Tom made after all.

Sean shoved away from his desk and paced the small room he used for an office. He'd done the best he could. He'd talked to Tom, hadn't he? Pointed out the places where he might come across as being disinterested. When a client brushed him off, he stayed brushed off. He wasn't going to run to the bride and plant seeds of doubt and suspicion. Usually, a word here or there in the guy's ear was enough to get them to click back in.

Sean's hands balled into fists.

He had too much to do to be wrapped up in personal drama. Drama he'd brought on himself. It wasn't as if Larissa was speaking to him, so why did it matter? He had to let this go. Move on. Stay busy.

That last one wouldn't be a problem. Not with Anna and Duncan getting married in fifteen days. He had to be insane for saying it could be done. Even more so for being a willing participant in it.

He glanced at his desk. There were heaps of things he should focus on, and yet . . . With a sigh, he headed to his bedroom to change. Everyone would be better off if he could collect his thoughts and put this madness with Larissa behind him. A run might not fix things completely, but it would help.

Something had to.

4

L arissa stacked boxes on the top of her trunk. She eyed the pile remaining in her back seat and sighed. "Fine. I'll do multiple trips."

She bumped the car door with her hip to close it and gathered the stack into her arms. Trying to peek around the boxes, she wound through the parking lot toward the shipping store and promptly tripped over the curb.

"Oh . . . fiddlesticks!" That wasn't the word she thought. Did she get any bonus points for not letting it slip out? She skipped, trying to find her balance, and two of the top boxes toppled off, landing with a thud on the asphalt. Another word she hadn't said in years flitted through her head. This was all Tom's fault. Every. Single. Bit.

Larissa blew out a breath and closed her eyes, trying to count away her anger, but the increasing numbers just stoked the fire. Finally, she let the curse word on the tip of her tongue out and kicked at one of the boxes.

"Need a hand?"

No. No no no. This was not happening. She pried open an

eye and peeked. Her anger drained away as hot embarrassment took its place. She cleared her throat. "Hi, Sean."

"Hi." He gathered the fallen boxes and looked at the stack she was holding. "How about I get these?"

"Yeah, okay. Thanks." She sounded ungrateful. There wasn't anything she could do about that, since she was. Mostly. All she'd wanted to do was get the gifts she'd been unable to return to the store shipped back to their givers. Then she could move on with the important things in her life.

"How's it going?"

"Really? How do you imagine it's going?"

Red tinted Sean's cheeks as he reached for the door of the shipping store. "Badly. But I wasn't sure what else to ask."

"Why are you even here?" Larissa stacked the boxes in her arms on the counter and reached for the two he carried. Why did such hateful words keep coming out of her mouth?

"I just met a couple at the coffee shop across the way—pre-consult." He set down the boxes and tucked his hands in his pockets. "I was walking to my car when I saw a woman trip, almost fall, and lose some boxes. I came over to help before I realized it was you."

Larissa nodded. Of course he had. Because Sean was a nice guy. The kind of guy who made a habit of climbing trees to rescue kittens. "Sorry."

He shrugged. "Do you have more in your car?"

Did the man know everything? "Of course I do. Because hardly any stores will take things back without receipts. Oh, sure, I could get store credit, but they won't transfer that to the giver, even though I could give them a name and address. So I have to ship it all back so people who've already gone out of their way to be generous can now make extra trips to return things."

"Does it help at all if I say some of them will keep it and use it for the next wedding gift they need?"

She caught her lower lip between her teeth. Did that help? "Not really."

"Give me your keys."

Larissa frowned.

"I'll go get the rest. You start this process." He nodded at the employee who waited patiently behind the counter eyeing the stack of boxes.

"Why not." Shoulders sagging, Larissa tugged her keys out of the side pocket of her purse.

"I won't be a minute." Sean took the keys and jingled them.

She nodded, forced a bright smile, and turned to the shipping store employee. "Sorry."

"No problem. How fast do you want these to ship?"

"Cheap. I'd like it to be cheap."

The girl nodded and slid the first box onto the scale.

Larissa looked around the store. Flat boxes were stacked against the wall, while packing tape and other miscellaneous shipping supplies hung on racks or sat on shelves. There was a wall of mailboxes for people who didn't want to use the post office but still needed a PO Box. The store was silent. Why wasn't there some music playing in the background? Her gaze traveled to the floor-to-ceiling windows that made up the front of the store and locked on Sean as he strode across the parking lot, the last of her boxes balanced in his arms with seeming ease.

She'd always found him attractive. Tom had given her a hard time about it the first time they'd all met. She'd rolled her eyes and reminded Tom that she was in love with *him*—still was. Wasn't she? Furious, sure, but being jilted hadn't magically erased the fact that she loved him. She'd been ready to spend the rest of her life with him. Didn't that count for something?

"Here you go." Sean set the stack of boxes next to the others.

The clerk's eyes widened, but she kept tapping at the computer.

"And your keys." He held them out.

"Thanks. All around, I guess."

"I can still help with the other details if you want."

"This is really it. When I got home on Sunday, I made a list. Gifts were the big thing."

"Did you have some you'd already opened or used?"

She nodded. She'd been against it, but Tom had convinced her they could start using stuff once the thank-you note was written. He'd taken all the towels and sheets to the apartment they'd planned to share. The one he'd already moved into since his lease was up three months ago. She still had two weeks on hers.

"What will you do about those?"

"I wrote checks and put them in the mail. I imagine most people would prefer I did that for everything, but I can't afford to."

Sean grinned. "Hey, you get some new stuff out of it, right?"

She gave a slight shake of her head before she thought better of it.

"What do you mean?"

Larissa sighed. "They're at Tom's. He took them home. Since that was going to be *our* home, it made sense. Less to move when we got back from our honeymoon. Which he has apparently gone on by himself."

"He did not." Fire lit in Sean's eyes and he gripped her arm. "Please tell me you're kidding."

Tears burned the back of her eyes. "I wish I was. It's all over his Instagram feed."

Sean's lips compressed and he looked away for a moment before turning back. His whole expression had gentled. "I'm so, so sorry."

"It's not your fault." She would've liked to continue to believe it was, but sometime over the last two days she'd been forced to see the truth.

The clerk cleared her throat. "Is there anything else I can help you with today?"

"No. That's everything, thanks." Larissa offered the woman her credit card without looking at the total. It's not like it mattered. She couldn't not ship anything. They all needed to go back to where they came from, even if it obliterated her budget for the month. She glanced at Sean out of the corner of her eye. Why was he still here? With a tight smile, she took the receipt. "Have a good day."

"Where are you off to now?" Sean held the door open for her and followed behind onto the sidewalk.

"Back to my apartment, I guess. I need to finish packing."

"Packing? Why are you packing? What'd I miss?"

"I gave notice two months ago that I was leaving when my lease is up. They've already rented it to someone else. Married or not, I have to be out in two weeks."

His jaw dropped and his eyebrows drew together. "That's unfair."

Larissa managed a harsh chuckle. "The whole situation is unfair. It's okay. I didn't love living there. Granted, I liked it more than I think I'm going to enjoy being homeless."

"You can find another place. There are ton of apartments in Richmond."

"Sure, but they mostly have a wait. There aren't many in my price range with immediate openings." Well, in her price range and in an area she was okay with. There were several options she was hesitantly considering. They were probably okay, but they weren't in great neighborhoods. If nothing else, they were better than being out on the street or trying to couch surf at friends' houses. A lot of her friendships were suffering from

Tom's behavior. She didn't know how many people she'd thought were friends would end up choosing him in the end. Just one more dagger in her heart.

"Let me take you to dinner."

"I—have—" What? She'd finished all her online English teaching for the day. She had an evening of packing waiting for her. She didn't even have a cat anymore, since Tom hadn't liked cats and had made her re-home Sassy. That should've been the first sign. Why hadn't she seen it?

Larissa studied Sean. What harm was there in having dinner with a friend? The fact that the friend was good-looking and male was a small balm to her aching soul. "You know what? That sounds nice. Thanks."

ON FRIDAY AFTERNOON, Larissa followed behind the last of the men she'd hired to load the portable storage pod that had been delivered early in the morning. She added her final box to it, closed the door, and locked it.

"That's it?"

She nodded and passed over an envelope thick with cash. He'd distribute it to his crew. In one tiny part of her mind, she questioned the legality of having hired them. They surely weren't taking payroll taxes out of the money she gave them, but she didn't have a lot of options. This was the least horrible one available. "Thank you."

The man nodded, touched the brim of his baseball cap, and chattered rapidly in Spanish at the two other men on the sidewalk. They responded, nodded to her, and headed toward the banged-up pickup they'd arrived in.

Larissa stared at the storage container in her second parking spot. The spot that usually held Tom's sleek sports car. She growled. When was she going to stop thinking about Tom? He hadn't spared a thought for her for the last week. That much was obvious from his social media feeds. Instead of nursing a broken heart on the cruise, it looked like he'd had the time of his life with an endless rotation of skinny blondes on his arm.

Maybe it was a good thing she had to move out. She'd find someplace where there weren't a thousand memories of Tom every time she turned around. Then perhaps she'd stop seeing a thousand examples of how unlovable she must be. She'd turned her life upside down for him, and it still hadn't been enough to make him stay.

Her cell rang as she unlocked her apartment door. Larissa frowned at the unfamiliar number. Since she'd filled out a number of contact forms for apartment complexes this week, she answered. *Please, God, if You still care anything about my life, let it be one of them with an opening.* "Hello?"

"Hi, Larissa? It's Claire McIntyre, from Peacock Hill."

So much for God caring. Hadn't her parents paid the final invoice? They'd told her they had everything under control. "Yeah, hi, Claire. What can I do for you?"

"Actually, I was hoping maybe I had something that could help you." Claire cleared her throat. "Sean mentioned to Anna that you were apartment shopping, but that it was looking like you'd have a gap between when you had to move out and when something reasonable would be available."

"Of course he did." Larissa sagged against the wall, then gave up and slid the rest of the way to the floor of the empty apartment.

"He's worried about you. Anyway, Anna mentioned it to me at breakfast and . . . well, why don't you come stay here?"

Too many thoughts battled for attention. Why was Sean worried? It's not as if they'd been friends forever. They'd been passing church acquaintances. Then they'd had a business relationship that had morphed into a friendship of sorts, the same kind of friendship he probably had with all his clients. For all she knew, he took every one of his clients out to dinner after their weddings—just it was usually a couple, not a heartbroken, jilted bride. Gah. She had to stop thinking about herself that way.

She dragged her focus to the other part of Claire's statement. Go live at Peacock Hill. Could she? "Um. How's the Internet there?"

Claire chuckled. "We've got high speed. There are wired connections in the business center, or we have wifi that works steadily in the rest of the house."

She could keep working. How to continue teaching online between residences had been her biggest worry. It wasn't as if she had a different job to fall back on. This was what she did, and it required Internet access. "I wouldn't be in the way?"

"Not even the slightest bit. We have a handful of individual retreats booked, but nothing that would fill us to capacity by any stretch. And with Anna and Duncan getting married soon, you could even choose a set of rooms on the third floor if you wanted. The rooms up there all have en suite bathrooms, so they're a better choice anyway."

Larissa chewed on her lower lip. It was tempting. So tempting. "When could I come?"

"As soon as you wanted. Today? Tomorrow? Just let us know."

She had to be here when they came to pick up her storage container, but that was scheduled for early tomorrow morning. "What furniture would I need? I just put everything in storage."

"You remember the room you stayed in last weekend? They're all set up like that."

Larissa heard the wince in Claire's voice when she mentioned the wedding. The room had been comfortable though. Bed, desk, good lighting, and even a little sitting area. It would work. "How much are you charging your retreat guests?"

"Oh, no. We weren't expecting—"

"Please. You're saving me settling for someplace I really don't want to live or a weekly-rate motel. Which is also a place I really don't want to live, given a choice. I can afford to pay rent." Or that was the theory. It depended on the rates they'd set.

Claire sighed and named a nightly price that was lower than Larissa expected. She did a quick mental calculation to make it weekly and frowned. It wasn't cheap, but it was still better than the rest of her options. Best of all, it would work in her budget with minimal tweaking. Bonus? She wouldn't see Tom in every room there, because he'd never managed to be free to attend any of their trips down.

"All right. I'll be out tomorrow afternoon. After four?"

"That sounds great. We'll look forward to seeing you. Think about whether you want to be on the second or third floor. Or you can wait and look at both options again if you'd rather. Either way. See you tomorrow."

"Yeah. Thanks, Claire."

"More than welcome, but it was really Sean's idea. Thank him. Bye."

Larissa ended the call and frowned at her phone. Sean's idea. Why did he care? He didn't have any reason to, not anymore. She tapped out a text thanking him and set her phone aside. She hadn't been able to reschedule the storage container delivery without a hefty fee. Even then, the company hadn't wanted to guarantee they could make a date closer to her move out work. So she'd gone ahead with it as planned. If there was an upside to Sean's thoughtfulness and the kindness of the ladies at Peacock Hill, it was that she'd only be spending one night in a pile of blankets on the floor instead of two weeks.

If she was leaving tomorrow, there was a lot of cleaning to

do. That, if nothing else, ought to keep her mind off Sean. Did he feel sorry for her? Somehow responsible? She blew out a breath and stood. He wasn't to blame. No matter how much she might wish he'd told her his concerns, the fact was if she'd seen the same behavior in a friend's fiancé, she would've known something was wrong. She'd been blind.

Tom leaving her at the altar was no one's fault but her own.

5

Sean watched the coffee drip into the pot. Why did it always take longer when he was exhausted? He scrubbed a hand over his face and tried to focus. He should have gone home after the wedding last night. Gone home and slept. Then he could've gone to church at his usual place of worship and driven out to Peacock Hill afterward. Sure, driving out last night had netted him an extra two hours— possibly three—with Duncan and Anna, but they weren't who had propelled him into his car.

Richmond seemed empty without Larissa.

Stupid stupid stupid. Stupid. He added a fourth for good measure.

She was grieving the loss of her marriage. Even if he believed it was the best thing that could have happened to her, the way it happened had to hurt. The last thing he wanted to be was her rebound guy. He wanted to be her forever guy.

Stupid.

And yet, here he was, dressed and ready for church at least an hour before anyone else would be up, watching the sloth-like coffeemaker at Peacock Hill because he didn't want to miss a chance to talk to Larissa.

When he judged enough coffee had drizzled into the carafe to fill a mug, he grabbed the handle and poured. A drop of coffee hissed on the burner before he could replace the glass container. Sean took a sip, burning his tongue on the bitter brew. But it woke him up. A little. Enough that now he could add sugar and cream without making a mess. It was his time-honed tradition.

More alert, he sipped at his doctored coffee at the small kitchen table and opened his Bible. The words blurred as the schedule for his upcoming week tried to clamor for his attention. Sean closed his eyes and worked to clear his mind, settling into a prayer for clarity and peace.

"What are you doing here?"

His eyes flew open at Larissa's voice.

She scowled at him from the doorway to the kitchen.

"And good morning to you, too." Sean reached for his mug and took a long swig. He shouldn't find her bedhead adorable, but he did. "Nine days. We're nine days out from Duncan and Anna's wedding. There's stuff to talk about and do that requires me to be present. So here I am, breaking my 'I don't work on Sunday' rule for friends."

Larissa looked away, pink staining her cheeks. "Sorry."

"There's coffee." Or there ought to be. The machine had enough time to work through another cupful, hadn't it?

"Thanks." She padded barefoot to the machine and got a mug from the cupboard above. "And thanks again for talking to Anna about me staying here. You shouldn't have."

Why not? Sean didn't ask. He wasn't sure he wanted to know her answer. She'd say something about them being casual friends at best and how he shouldn't do stuff like that for random clients, because it was too much. That's the lecture his mother had given him. Dad hadn't said much. Dad tended to see the subtext that went over Mom's head, which meant Sean had gotten a call from his father later, reminding him that falling in love with brides-to-be was a bad business plan. "It came up in conversation. She's the one who called and invited you."

Larissa looked over her shoulder at him and shook her head.

What did that mean? He'd been very clear the invitation needed to come from Claire. Whatever. He couldn't fix anything at this point, so he'd do what he always did when he hit an unexpected snag. He'd roll with it. "How are you settling in?"

"I got here yesterday afternoon. I've managed to unload my car and schlep stuff up two enormous flights of stairs. I always thought high ceilings were grand. Then I had to climb the stairs that go with them." She flopped into a seat across from him. "I'm redesigning my dream home to have six foot ceilings."

Sean chuckled. "Why didn't you use the elevator?"

"There's an elevator? Of course there is. Where? At least I can use it when I leave."

"I'm surprised they didn't point it out. I'll show you after coffee. It's behind a door, so it looks like a closet, but it makes toting things up and down a lot easier."

"Jeremiah was the only one around when I got here, and he was on his way out. He just said choose a room and welcome." Larissa shrugged and lifted her mug, holding it near her face for several seconds before sipping. "I guess the exercise was good."

"That's the spirit. Plus it's only one flight."

She shook her head. "I'm on three."

Sean frowned into his coffee. Hadn't that been designated the men's floor? Had he spent last night in the room next to hers? He'd chosen a random room from the open doors, falling into bed without looking around. But he couldn't stay. Not now he knew she was up there. Could he?

Something of his thoughts must have shown on his face.

Larissa was defensive. "They said it was okay. Those rooms are all *en suite*, and a little bigger, actually. With Duncan and Anna moving into their cottage next week. I know how to lock my door, but I also don't think Duncan has any nefarious plans."

"Of course he doesn't. I was surprised is all. It makes sense to get a room with a bathroom." Was he forever going to undo any progress he made with her by speaking first and thinking second? Not that he was looking to make progress. She was about as off-limits as they got. At least for a while. She needed to heal. He needed to let her. Time to change the subject. "You heading to church with the gang?"

"Wasn't planning on it. I'm reasonably certain God doesn't care what I do."

Sean set his coffee down with a thunk. At least it was almost empty, so nothing sloshed over the side. "Larissa . . . no. You know that's a lie."

She lifted a shoulder and stared out the window behind him. "I'm not so sure. Look at me. I'm nearing thirty. I spent four years of my life with the man I was positive God intended me to marry, and then he couldn't be bothered to show up for our wedding. Now all my worldly goods are locked in a metal box in a stack of identical metal boxes and I can't get to them without paying an exorbitant fee, so if I happen to remember something I need, I'm out of luck. I live in a single room—with a bathroom, and I should acknowledge that positive—in an enormous house owned by strangers that is, hilariously, where I'd hoped to start my life with the man I didn't realize didn't love me until it was too late. What part of any of that is God caring about my life?"

Sean choked back his impulse to point out the positives she did have. Now wasn't the time. At best, she'd call him Pollyanna. At worst, she'd never want to speak to him again. He wasn't risking that. "I'm sorry."

"Not your fault."

"I'm still sorry. Is there any way I can help?"

Larissa drained her coffee and stood. "Sure. Go on to church and tell God that if He expects me to love Him, then He'd better show up. 'Cause I'm tired of loving people who aren't there when I need them to be."

Sean's heart broke a little as she stormed from the room. The swinging kitchen door didn't slam, but it kept moving back and forth long enough that he could guess at the force she'd used on it.

He closed his eyes and started to pray.

"Where's that new girl who's living up at the Hill with you?" Mrs. Patterson's eyes scanned the crowd before returning to Sean. She frowned. "Are you living up there now, too?"

"No, ma'am. I'm just down to work with Duncan and Anna on their wedding."

The woman sniffed. "I don't agree with the hurry. Everyone's going to be watching for a baby bump over the summer. If there's no reason to rush, they ought to take their time."

Sean bristled. "They've been engaged since September, and I believe they decided—"

"There you are, Sean. Good morning, Mrs. Patterson. It's nice to see you and Jim back from your travels." Duncan shook the woman's hand with a genuine smile. "You'll be at the wedding next Tuesday, I hope? Matt said you weren't leaving town again until June?"

Mrs. Patterson smiled at the mention of Matt's name. She was his aunt, was that right? At least she had a kind word for someone.

"That's right. Of course, we'll be back in time for Matt and Azure to marry over Labor Day weekend. Jim'll run the garage for a bit while they take a honeymoon. Have you and Anna figured out your wedding trip?"

"We're going to stay here. The cottage at the back of the garden is cozy enough and we can't take the time just now. We'll plan to get away after Thanksgiving to do something special." Duncan shifted his attention to Sean. "Should we plan to pick up lunch for Larissa since she's not feeling well?"

Sean watched Mrs. Patterson's interest perk when she heard that. Bless Duncan. At least Larissa had an excuse for one Sunday. "I think Deidre said she'd take care of it, since she and Jeremiah were headed home and the three of us were going to Charlottesville. That's still the plan?"

Duncan nodded. "Just wanted to be sure. It's easy enough to make a stop on the way if needed. Anna's finishing up downstairs with some of the kids. Then we'll be ready to go."

"You tell your young lady that I hope we'll see her in church next weekend." Mrs. Patterson patted Sean's arm. "I imagine we'll be seeing more of you now she's staying here."

Words clogged in Sean's throat. "I—we're not—Larissa isn't—"

"Isn't she?" Mrs. Patterson smiled and faded into the crowded foyer.

Sean stared after her. That couldn't be what people thought. When had the woman even seen him with Larissa? He searched his memory and came up empty.

Duncan's chuckle broke Sean's reverie. "Gotta love Matt's aunt. Don't let her get to you. She was fishing. She likes to see people paired off."

"Right. Great." Sean scanned the crowd for the older woman. How did she disappear like that? "I'll go wait in the car."

WEDNESDAY, and Sean was ready to tear his hair out.

How could two people whose entire livelihood revolved around plants not be able to provide the flowers for their own wedding? Oh, sure, Anna hadn't thought it would be a problem a week and a half ago. But now she didn't have time. They'd taken on a big new job, one that could do great things for their fledgling business. Great. Good for them. Sean was trying to do great things for their fledgling wedding.

No one seemed to care.

Growling, he flipped through his book of vendors. Didn't any florists owe him favors? He ran a finger down the list and slowed. He paused and tapped a name. She didn't owe him, not really, but she liked him. He pressed his fingers to his eyes. He'd stopped using Vanessa for flowers primarily because she liked him.

She was a flirt and had a hard time taking no for an answer. It was an embarrassing challenge to coordinate and set up a wedding when the florist crossed all kinds of professional lines. But Vanessa was a brilliant florist and easy and straightforward to work with. When she wanted to be.

"Duncan and Anna better appreciate this." Sean continued to mutter as he punched in Vanessa's number. He quieted when it began to ring and forced a smile.

"Best Buds, this is Vanessa."

"Hi, Vanessa. It's Sean Fitzgerald."

"Sean. Wow, it's been a while." Vanessa giggled. "How are you?"

Sean cringed. Giggles had to be the world's deadliest sound. Even the word sounded stupid. "I'm great, thanks. Listen, I've got a last-minute wedding I'm trying to pull together for some friends and I was hoping you could help."

"You know I'd do anything for you. Why don't you come by the shop and we can work everything out?"

"Don't you even want to know when I need the flowers?" Was her business going so badly it didn't matter? If that was the case, maybe he needed to keep looking. In the past, her arrangements had always been perfect, but time could change things.

"Of course I do, but I'll make it work because it's you. Unless it's tomorrow. I can't do tomorrow. We're slammed and there are only so many hours in the day." All the flirting disappeared, replaced with a brisk, businesslike tone. "It's not tomorrow, right?"

"No. Not tomorrow. Tuesday."

"As in . . ." She counted under her breath. "Six days away? That Tuesday?"

"That's the one."

She sighed, her breath crackling in his ear. "I can make it work, but it's going to cost and you're going to be limited to what we have on hand or I can get fast. Nothing exotic. You really need to come by the shop."

Sean's smile was real this time. "It's a simple wedding, so I'm sure we'll be able to work it out. I can be there around two. Does that work?"

Papers rustled in the background. "Two's okay, but I'll need to work while we talk."

"Fair enough. I appreciate this, Vanessa."

"It'll be fun to see you again." The flirtatious tone returned. He ended the call and sighed. With luck, he'd be able to keep her so focused on the tight turnaround that she wouldn't lapse back into crazy while he was there.

6

L arissa closed her browser and leaned back, rolling her head on her neck. The business center at Peacock Hill was cozy and quiet, but the chairs weren't amazing for long stretches of time. She stood and reached her arms up over her head until her shoulders popped.

"Ouch."

Larissa turned, chuckling when she saw Anna. "Not really. It just sounds bad. You need me?"

"No. The printer. Sean sent us some stuff from the florist. I need to print it and make some choices, then email it back today." Anna checked her phone. "In like an hour."

"Nothing like the last minute." Larissa smiled to soften her words. She didn't want to make the girl feel bad, but it was surprising how little . . . care she seemed to be putting into her big day. "Can I see?"

Anna hooked her phone to the printer and started tapping. "Sure. I wouldn't even mind opinions, if you have them. Duncan gave me his thoughts, and they basically match mine, but I'm starting to second-guess myself."

"Then I'm your girl. I loved picking out the flowers for my

wedding." The pain was a swift, sudden stab. Larissa caught her breath and waited for it to ease. She forced her lips to curve. "It's an exciting time, isn't it?"

Anna frowned at her phone then checked the connection to the printer. "I know it's supposed to be. I guess I still wonder why we couldn't elope. Quick trip to the courthouse and done, you know?"

"I really don't." On the other hand, maybe if she and Tom had done that eighteen months ago when they got engaged, she'd be married now. But would it be a happy marriage? It was a question she didn't know how to answer. Up until last week, it wasn't something she would even have asked. They'd done pre-marital counseling. They were friends underneath the love and physical attraction. Every book, every mentor, suggested had done everything right. Except for that part where the reality of being married to her had been such a terrible thing to face, Tom ran the other direction. Not about her. This was about Anna. "You didn't play wedding as a little girl?"

"Maybe once? Oh, finally." The printer started spitting papers. Anna gathered them up as they came out. When the machine stopped, she pulled a chair over to an empty stretch of desk. "All right. We're working with what's in her coolers and not already spoken for, plus a short list of things she thinks she can get quickly."

Larissa looked over the papers Anna laid out. The florist wasn't one Sean had taken her to, but the photos of the samples were beautiful. "Simple, right? Did you choose colors?"

"Sort of? I said spring colors—but I wanted to leave it open to pastels or some of the brighter candy colors. I love the riot of blooms in a garden when it starts to open. I'd love to re-create something like that."

Hmm. Larissa eyed the papers again then tapped a basket that gave off that vibe of spring. It was casual. A far cry from the formal arrangements Larissa had ordered for herself. But it suited Anna and Duncan. It'd go just as well with jeans as it would Sunday best. Even with more formal clothes, it'd be like the goofy uncle who gets invited along to keep things from being stuffy. "These."

"You think?" Anna's eyes brightened. "I really like those, but we're still going formal for the wedding party. Aren't they too fun?"

Larissa laughed. "You can have fun in formal clothes. And if you want to emphasize joy, these are going to help set that tone."

"They will, won't they?" Anna squealed and clapped her hands. "Thank you! I wasn't sure if I could veer away from the expected."

"It's your wedding. You can do whatever you want." Within the limits of their budget and time constraints. And what Duncan would agree to. But none of that seemed worth mentioning in the face of Anna's glow. "Will Duncan like them?"

"Yes, I'm pretty sure he will. He said he liked them all at first, and only settled on this other one when I pushed. I think he was trying to choose what he thought I'd choose, you know?"

She didn't. The few times Tom had had an opinion on their wedding plans, he'd made it clear that she'd better agree with his choice. They'd had a huge fight the one time she'd tried to get him to compromise. He'd stormed off and hadn't spoken to her for two days. Even then, he'd only thawed because she'd apologized and they'd gone with his idea. He hadn't shown much interest in the plans after that. Larissa hadn't pushed.

"Thanks for this, Larissa. I'm so glad you're here." Anna gave her a fast side hug. "I'm going to run and check this with Duncan then shoot it off to the florist. You're coming on Tuesday, right?"

She hadn't planned to. She barely knew these people. "I have work."

"Pfft. You can take a couple hours off, can't you? Please?" Anna clutched the papers to her chest and smiled so hopefully, Larissa didn't have the heart to say no.

"I'll rearrange some stuff."

Anna grinned. "Yay! Thanks again."

When Anna left, Larissa sagged into her chair. She should've seen the problems with Tom. How had she missed them? Had she been so focused on finally getting her perfect wedding that she hadn't cared whether or not the man standing with her was the right one? No. She'd loved Tom. She'd believed she understood God's will for the two of them—which proved she had no clue. Or that God didn't care. The jury was still out on that. Saying God didn't care aloud to Sean had left everything in her quivering. She'd had too many years of church, too many years of striving to be who God wanted her to be, to put the full force of her faith behind the statement. But thinking it was getting easier.

She had an hour before her next student expected her. She'd go take a stroll through the gardens and clear her head.

LARISSA STOOD at the base of a round stone tower and stared up at the peaked top. What was it? She glanced over her shoulder. She could just see the roof of the main house, though most of the view was blocked by a copse of trees. She'd wandered through the formal gardens and around the lake, tempted by the benches settled in secluded nooks, but hadn't stopped until she saw this. It was ridiculously out of place, like some sort of medieval relic dropped onto the property though a rip in space and time. She snorted out a laugh. At least she still found herself amusing.

"Out for a walk?"

Larissa nodded and hurried through the list of names for the women at Peacock Hill. "Azure, right?"

"That's me." She nodded toward the tower. "Checking out the weird?"

"It's not what I expected to find." Larissa shrugged. "But it's pretty."

"That it is. I'm hoping Deidre will take my suggestion and turn it into a guest cottage. Wouldn't it be fun to live in something like this for a week?"

A week? Larissa eyed the structure. There were probably three or four floors in the thing, but none were more than what, fifteen feet in diameter? At best. "It's small."

Azure chuckled. "I used to live in a small travel trailer. This would be palatial in comparison. Want to go in? I've got a key."

"Why?"

"Why would you want to go in, or why do I have a key?"

"The key. Not that it's any of my business. Obviously. You know what? I should go. I have another class starting soon anyway." Larissa's cheeks burned. No wonder Tom had left her. She probably sent people running all the time without even realizing it.

"When you have some time, if you want to go up, come find me. I'm either in town at Matt's garage, or I'm that way," Azure pointed past the tower toward the forest. "There's a clearing. I like to paint there when I can. And Deidre gave me a key because I nagged her about it. She said if I could come up with a legitimate way to make the tower livable, she'd listen."

"Cool." It was the safest reply Larissa could manage. She didn't want to stick her foot in her mouth any more than she already had. She knew Azure lived in one of the rooms on the second floor. They might share a residence, but Larissa hadn't run into the woman since she'd moved down. "I guess I'll see you."

"I'll walk back with you, if you don't mind. At least some of the way. I want to stop by Anna and Duncan's cottage. Anna was supposed to be there this afternoon and I thought she might want some help." Azure shrugged and fell into step beside Larissa. "Matt's got the garage under control, and I needed some air."

"You're engaged to Matt, right?" It seemed like everyone at Peacock Hill was engaged or married. The notable exception was Deidre's sister, Claire. And Claire seemed like she was in the same "men are pigs" camp Larissa currently inhabited. "Got a date?"

"Labor Day weekend." Azure slid her hands into the pockets of her brightly painted overalls. "It seems like a million years away in some ways, and like tomorrow in others."

Larissa nodded. The feeling was familiar. "Is Sean Fitzgerald helping you plan things?"

"Yeah. Figured it didn't hurt to have a professional point us in the right direction. We're keeping it simple, though. A little ceremony at the church, then back here for a cookout in the gardens. Labor Day, right? You have to have hamburgers."

They rounded the bend on the gravel path and the small, two-story wooden cottage greeted them. Larissa paused. How had she missed this before? She glanced back the way she'd come and frowned. She'd crossed through the garden paths and missed the fact that there was a gravel path—almost like a road —that appeared to circle the property.

"It's like something out of a fairy tale."

Azure grinned. "Isn't it? I'm not sure what they'll do when they start a family, but for now it's the perfect little house. You want the tour? I'm sure Anna would show you around."

Larissa checked the time on her phone and shook her head. "I have to get back. Maybe I could see both places this weekend, if the two of you are around."

"Sure. Saturday's usually pretty busy at the garage, but we close at two unless we have a call. So maybe around three?"

"Okay." What was she going to do with her weekends stuck in this tiny town? She lifted her fingers in a brief wave before heading back toward the main house. It wasn't like she had to stay here. She could drive back to Richmond and do something. Or Charlottesville, which was closer. Or she could head west and see what lay in that direction. Maybe she could learn to enjoy hiking.

She wrinkled her nose. No. That wasn't going to happen. There'd been almost too much nature for her just strolling the garden paths on the grounds here. There'd been bugs. Bees. Spiderwebs, which inevitably meant spiders, though she hadn't seen any. She also hadn't looked. For all she knew, there were snakes hiding in the undergrowth.

Larissa shuddered as she headed back inside. Richmond might not be a huge city, but she missed it. After her class, she was spending more time apartment hunting. Right now, her best option had a six-month waiting list.

There was no way she'd survive six months in the sticks.

7

S ean peeked around the corner and down into the sunken garden where Anna and Duncan had decided to hold the ceremony. It wasn't a large space, maybe fifty feet on each side of the square. The large fish-shaped fountain in the center burbled cheerily while creating a focal point that wasn't the bride and groom. He frowned. This wasn't a venue he would have suggested, but their hearts were set on it. They'd shared some story on Sunday about how refurbishing the fountain played an integral part in the two of them getting together. But he'd been distracted, searching for any hint of Larissa. He hadn't seen her then, nor had he seen her yesterday. It made no sense. She lived and worked here, so why hadn't he bumped into her?

He'd been counting on it.

Focus, Sean. Focus.

Duncan and the minister were in place next to an enormous planting of bamboo in the far corner of the garden. They'd elected not to have attendants, so the other residents of Peacock Hill—Deidre, Jeremiah, and Claire—were seated with a handful of other guests. He spotted Mrs. Patterson, dressed in her finest, while the gentleman next to her looked uncomfortable in a dark suit and bright red tie. That had to be Mr. Patterson. Poor man. Most of the other faces were familiar, but putting names to them might take a minute.

He didn't see Larissa.

Hadn't Anna said she was coming?

"Am I late? I'm not late, right?"

Sean turned and something in his chest loosened as his gaze fell on Larissa. She wore a floral dress that looked like something out of a 1950s garden party. Her white short-sleeved sweater only added to the impression that she ought to have bobby socks and sneakers on instead of the slim heels that matched the pale green in the leaves on her skirt. He swallowed. "You're not late, but you're lovely."

Pink stole across her cheeks. "I'm sure everyone is. Do I just sit anywhere?"

He nodded. "I think there's room by . . . oh, what's her name? The painter?"

"Azure?" Larissa craned her head around the corner and nodded. "I see it. Thanks, Sean."

"Sure." She'd already started down the steps and probably hadn't heard him. Which was fine. Gosh, she was pretty. And the hollowness that had seemed to hang around her like a cloud last week was gone. Or at least diminished. That was good.

"Are we ready?"

This time it was Anna sneaking up on him from behind. He grinned. "You look great."

She stroked the simple A-line skirt of her tea-length gown. The intricate beading on the bodice elevated it from plain to stunning. Sean hadn't been sold on the idea of online wedding dress shopping, but he was happy to have been proven wrong.

"You're set? Where are your flowers?" Sean frowned. Anna was supposed to be carrying five long-stemmed pale pink roses tied with a light green satin bow.

Her hand flew to her mouth and she glanced over her shoulder. "I left them inside."

"I'll go. You stay right here. And no peeking. If they see you, they're going to want to start and you'll ruin the effect." Sean pointed at her until she nodded. He loped across the front of the house and up the stairs. Inside, he scanned the foyer. No flowers. He hurried into the smaller room off on the left and nearly smacked into Vanessa. "Good. You're just who I was looking for."

A slow smile spread across her lips. "Oh? That's good to hear."

Sean gave an impatient shake of his head. "Anna's flowers. Where are they?"

"The bridal bouquet? I gave it to her when she was heading upstairs to get dressed."

"Seriously? Beforehand?"

Vanessa huffed. "I'm only one person. I needed to get the arrangements outside in place and then start working on the additions to the lawn so they're ready for the reception."

"Right. Fine. Upstairs?"

She nodded.

Great. It wasn't like this was an enormous house with like twenty rooms on three floors or anything. He took the steps on the grand staircase by twos. He had no idea which room was Anna's, so he started trying doorknobs. After quick glances in four rooms, he finally spotted the flowers tossed on a bed with a pair of jeans and, good grief, undergarments. Did no one pick up after themselves? Averting his eyes from the lacy garments, he grabbed the flowers and jogged back to the stairs. He checked his watch. Only five minutes behind schedule. It could be worse.

"Did you—"

Sean waved the blooms at Vanessa as he raced through the foyer, mentally adding another reason not to work with Vanessa again if he could avoid it. Who gave out the bouquets that far in advance? No one, that's who. Well, no one but Vanessa. She had come through for him on short notice. He had to give her that. But otherwise? Disaster. As usual.

Panting, Sean arrived at the garden entrance and thrust the flowers into Anna's hands. "Here. Now. Ready?"

She grinned and sniffed the blooms. "Take a breath. It's fine."

His smile was tight. "We're behind. I don't want anyone thinking you're not going to show. That'd kill the Peacock Hill wedding business in about two minutes flat."

Anna chuckled and patted Sean's arm. "It's okay."

"Great. Right." He took a deep breath and finally regained control of his lungs. "Then let's get this wedding started."

There wasn't room for any sort of live musician in the sunken garden, so they'd settled on recordings. Sean lowered the volume of the prelude music, skipped to the bridal entrance track on the CD, and turned the speakers back up. Anna stepped to the top of the stairs and everyone stood.

Sean glanced between Duncan and Anna. His lips curved. It was good to see people in love making a commitment to one another. So many people today skipped this step. He had friends who loudly decried the need for "another piece of paper" as they put it. They were committed to one another, they said, and no ceremony could change that. Except it did. There was something reverent and holy about a wedding. It's what kept him in the business on days when clients went crazy and nothing seemed to be going right.

Anna's parents stood and spoke quietly, giving her away. It was different, but it worked. Anna hadn't wanted to count on her parents being able to make the trip out from California, so she'd not planned for anyone to walk her down the aisle. Plus there wasn't really an aisle. It was good they'd found a way to involve her parents.

He checked his watch. He had just enough time to zip up to

the main lawn and check on the reception setup before they'd need him again for music. The photographer crouched to the side, snapping photos of the bride and groom. Everything here seemed to be well under control.

Raised voices greeted him as he strode past the marble lion fountain facing the back of the house. He picked up his pace.

"If I'd wanted them there, I would have put them there. You had no right to move them!" Vanessa clutched a planter of flowers to her chest and scowled at the caterer.

Sean sighed. He should have known if there drama broke out that Vanessa would be involved. "What's going on? And can we keep it down and talk like reasonable adults? I could almost hear you at the ceremony."

"This woman," Topher pointed at Vanessa, "put flowers where the cake is meant to go."

Sean pinched the bridge of his nose. "I sent both of you a layout diagram for this space on Friday. Who didn't get it?"

Neither spoke.

"So you both got it?"

Both managed hesitant nods.

"So?" Sean fished his phone out of his pocket and pulled up the diagram. He scanned the setup. "Topher, that's not where catering is supposed to be."

Vanessa shot Topher a triumphant look.

"Do you see the sun?" Topher gestured to the sky. "I can put the cake there if you want, but it's going to melt before anyone gets to see it."

Sean frowned. That was a valid point. He hadn't considered that when he'd drawn the diagram. He looked over to where Topher was in the process of setting up. It was the best spot for the food. "Okay. The design is bad, you stay put. Vanessa, you'll need to move the plants. Can you put them here, where the cake was going to go?"

"It's not big enough. It'll get lost."

"Work with me, Vi. Please?" Sean glanced at the time. He had maybe three minutes before he needed to book it back to the ceremony. The service was short and sweet, with very little planned beyond the basics. Even the homily was under ten minutes.

She sighed. "I'll make it work. But he isn't to move any more of my flowers without asking first."

"Topher?" Sean sent the caterer a pleading look.

Topher rolled his eyes. "Whatever."

"Thanks, man. Thanks, Vi." Sean glanced around the rest of the space. The tables were set in case anyone wanted to sit, but mostly it was a casual place to chat with friends and congratulate the couple while eating cake and drinking punch. There wasn't any other food planned. Sean figured people would stay a half hour. Tops. Maybe that's what Anna and Duncan wanted. "I have to get back. Call if you run into issues. On my phone. Not screaming."

Topher laughed.

Vanessa blushed.

Sean broke into a jog.

THE SUN WAS JUST BEGINNING to stain the sky a combination of pink and orange when the last guest headed for the stairs leading them to the house and out to the parking area. Sean blew out a breath and grinned. Even the prospect of another hour of cleanup couldn't change the fact the wedding had been a rousing success.

Duncan and Anna stood at the top of the stairs and waved before turning and matching Sean's grin with their own.

"That went well." Duncan slipped his arm around Anna's waist. She dropped her head to his shoulder and nodded.

"Thank you, Sean. We couldn't have done it without you. It was perfect." Anna tipped her head up and smiled at Duncan. "Don't you think?"

Duncan nodded.

Sean chuckled. "I see you've already perfected the art of agreeing with your wife."

"Well, it's easy when she's right." Duncan pressed a kiss to her forehead. "Can we help clean up?"

"No. Absolutely not. Frankly, I expected you two to be the first to leave, not the last."

Duncan shrugged. "No plane to catch. No long stretch of road ahead of us. Might as well hang out and enjoy the cake and our friends."

"Who you'll see again tomorrow." Sean shook his head. If it had been him, he would have at least planned an evening away. It didn't seem right to spend their first night as husband and wife at home.

"Maybe the day after. We're not planning on doing much tomorrow."

"Duncan!" Anna's face turned red and she jabbed her elbow into Duncan's belly.

Duncan laughed. "We *are* married."

"That doesn't mean you need to be crass."

Sean cleared his throat. "Why don't the two of you head on home? I've got this. Congratulations again. Thanks for letting me be part of your day."

Smiling, arms still wrapped around one another, Duncan and Anna headed toward the cottage that would be their home going forward. Sean allowed himself one wistful sigh before turning back to the last task of his evening. He hadn't hired help. With a wedding this small and a menu limited to cake and punch, there hadn't seemed to be a need.

Topher was busy packing up his dishes. Vanessa had disappeared. She was leaving the flowers, but they needed to be moved inside. Maybe she was starting with the sunken garden. Didn't matter. Sean pulled a tablecloth off the table nearest him, gave it a hard shake, and folded it. He dropped the cloth on one of the folding chairs then tipped the round table up on its edge so he could collapse the legs. He'd roll them down the slope and make a stack near the driveway so he could pull the van up and load them in all at once. It was the reverse of the process he'd used to get them up here this morning. There were only five tables, so it shouldn't take too long.

"Need a hand?"

Sean turned, frowning as his gaze landed on Larissa. "I've got it. Where'd you disappear to?"

She shrugged and started pulling chairs away from one of the tables anyway. "I had another class. I rearranged enough to be there for the ceremony but skipped the reception. It was for friends. I'm nobody."

"I wouldn't put it like that." He reached over to rest his hand on her arm. "Maybe you aren't one of their friends—yet—but I think if you let them, they'd add you to the group."

"I don't really need pity friends, but thanks." Larissa hefted the table onto its edge and began to fold the legs.

"Let me get that."

She slapped at his hands. "I can do it."

Sean bit back a remark. Something was going on with her. Did he even want to know what it was? Would she tell him, or did she consider him a pity friend as well? "You going to roll it down to the house as well?"

"Yep." She shot him a defiant look.

Alrighty then. It wasn't a big deal. Plus it meant he didn't have to do them all. Might as well find the bright side. Maybe then Larissa would spill whatever was bothering her. If there was a way for him to help, he would. He grabbed the table he'd already folded off the chairs he'd leaned it against. "This way."

Sean didn't check behind him to make sure she was managing the steep descent. It didn't seem like a great idea. Not with how prickly she'd been and how insistent she was about helping. Maybe she needed to prove something—to herself? To him? Hopefully it'd work either way.

When he reached the bottom of the hill, he propped his table against the low stone wall beside the driveway and turned to check on Larissa's progress. Her table wobbled and she lunged to keep it from dropping. From the dirt and grass on its top, Sean figured it had fallen at least once. She hadn't said a thing.

As she neared the bottom of the hill, her foot slipped. The table clattered to the ground as she landed on her rear.

"Are you all right?" Sean sprinted to close the distance between them and shoved the table out of the way. "Did it land on you?"

"I'm fine. It's fine." She pushed herself up and dusted off the back of her pants. "You're fast."

He snorted out a laugh. "Sure. I can move fast when I have visions of someone getting crushed by a table. Otherwise? Not really. You're sure you're okay?"

"The only thing hurt was my pride. Although this is pretty minor, given what you've seen happen to me."

Sean bent to grab the table. "It's good you're able to joke about it already."

"I'm not, not really. It's . . . laugh or cry, you know?" Larissa scrubbed at her palm.

He tucked the table under his arm and grabbed her hand. Blood welled in several small abrasions in the heel of her palm.

"Ooh. We should clean that, get you a bandage. Come on. I bet there's a first aid kit in the house."

"I'll get it. You can finish the cleanup. I'm not as helpful as I hoped I would be." Larissa looked away.

Sean rolled the table to the driveway and leaned it against the one he'd brought down. "I'm coming with. The tables and chairs aren't going anywhere."

"Don't be ridiculous. It's a scrape. I'm not dying." Larissa waved her hand toward the hill. "Go take care of your stuff."

He hesitated. She was right. She could handle her own first aid. And it was likely she'd run into someone inside if she needed help. There were plenty of people around. "Yeah, okay. I'll catch you before I leave."

Larissa turned and headed toward the house without comment. What did that mean?

It meant he was overthinking, that's what it meant. He jogged up the hill to the grassy area they'd used for the reception and made short work of collapsing the other tables. When they, plus the chairs, were staged against the low stone wall, Sean frowned at the house. She was in there. Had she washed out her scrape? Of course she had. He should go get the van, load everything up, and get going. Larissa was a big girl. She wasn't his problem.

Deliberately, he turned and strode toward the side of the house. He'd parked the van out of the way. It was a habit. Most wedding venues preferred the help to be invisible. It had never been an issue here at Peacock Hill. They treated him like family. They did that for everyone. But maybe he'd gotten too comfortable, letting his heart get involved with Larissa when there didn't seem to be any possible way for there to be something between them.

Sean pulled the van around the back to where he'd stacked the tables and chairs and made short work of loading everything. He stared at the house and turned away, heading up the hill to give the reception area one final look. He might have missed something—people left the strangest things at wedding receptions. This one hadn't been a rowdy party—with those, he half expected to find at least a shoe when he did his final sweep —but it was still worth looking.

It didn't look as if anything had happened on the lawn. Vanessa and Topher were gone. The fact he'd avoided bloodshed between them was a decided personal victory. Still, he'd try to avoid situations where they ended up working the same wedding. They were—what was worse than oil and water? Fertilizer and fire. Wasn't that what the terrorists used sometimes?

Now what?

His gaze strayed back to the house and he frowned. This was ridiculous. He'd swing by, check that Larissa was fine, and then head back to Richmond. Maybe, if he lucked out, he could avoid making a complete fool out of himself in the process.

8

L arissa pressed the last strip of medical tape to her palm with a grimace. Leave it to her to get a scrape big enough that standard bandages were too small. At least they'd had gauze pads and tape. Maybe she could have fit three of the regular strips together, but then she'd have to deal with the little sticky strip between each one still hitting her cut. Just no. So, old school it was, even if it made her look ridiculous.

She flexed her fingers, then made a fist. At least it didn't impede her ability to use her hands. Teaching online meant she did a lot of typing.

"I see you found the first aid kit."

Larissa turned and bit back a sigh. Of course it was Sean. "Yep. Right where you said it'd be."

"Everything okay?"

"Sure. Of course. You're all cleaned up?" Better—much better—to turn the conversation back to him.

He nodded and tucked his hands in his pockets. "I'm heading back to Richmond. It was good to see you."

Her heart thudded once at something almost wistful in his tone. Except that was ridiculous. He had to be tired after the day he'd put in. "Good to see you, too. I'm sure you'll be back this way before much longer."

"Maybe. I don't have any events scheduled out here for a while, and free time is a laughable idea until late August. My phone and my book are in the car, so I can't check, but that's what sticks in my head."

"Book? You use a paper calendar?"

Red crept up Sean's neck. "What can I say? I'm old school. I embraced technology like a fiend when I first started. Then there was a hardware failure and bam. Sixteen weddings got a lot more complicated. Since then? Paper backup at all times. You never noticed this when we were planning your wedding?"

Larissa waited for the stab of pain at the reminder of her wedding. It didn't come. The ache remained—the ache would likely always remain—but shouldn't someone talking about her public humiliation bring it all back? What did it mean if she'd gotten over Tom's desertion this fast? "I didn't, no. I seem to recall you using a tablet."

"I guess I do in meetings. Then I go home and transfer my notes and appointments to paper. I'm weird. I realize that."

"Whatever works. You put on a good wedding. I've been to two of them now—two vastly different events—you're good at your job. It's surprising."

"Why?"

"I guess—I mean, you're a guy, right? My folks were concerned about me hiring a man as a wedding planner. I think they assumed you'd be—" She searched for the right word that was less offensive than how her parents had phrased it.

"Flamboyant?" Sean sighed. "I get that a lot. For the record, not gay."

"I know that. My parents do too, for that matter. But you have to admit it's an unusual choice for a man."

He gave a slow nod. "It is. I didn't start out thinking I'd be a wedding planner. I started out helping my parents—my mom, mostly—plan events for several charities she worked with. I always enjoyed it, so when they asked if I'd help plan our high school graduation party, I agreed. I made extra money all through college helping out with campus events and got a bit of a reputation for knowing my way around event planning, so when my roommate and his fiancée asked if I'd plan their wedding, I thought why not? I left that reception having set up appointments with four other couples. It snowballed from there, but I love it. I should run. I have three dress fittings and two venue tours tomorrow."

Her eyebrows lifted. That was a lot. He'd never seemed hurried when she'd worked with him. They'd gone over their appointment times more often than not. He'd never said a word. He must build a lot of flex into his schedule to keep things running. "Busy day. Have fun."

"No point in doing it if I'm not." He winked and strode from the room.

Larissa rubbed away the little flutter in her belly. Better not to even try to analyze that. She was probably hungry. She'd pack up the first aid kit, fix herself a sandwich, and find something to do with herself. The long evening stretched out in front of her like a dark tunnel. She could watch TV. Read a book. Maybe even magically figure out what she was supposed to be doing with her life.

"I'M SO glad you decided to join us." Claire patted the seat next to her. "Sit here—it can be the singles section."

"Can it be a section when it's just two people?" Larissa snagged a bottle of root beer out of the cooler at the end of the long dining room table before moving down toward Claire.

"Maybe not, but I'm going with it. Matt and Azure should be here with the pizzas soon enough. Then the married couples will show up, and before you know it—"

"We'll be fifth wheels?" Larissa wrinkled her nose. Why had she agreed to this? A couple of friends in Richmond had begged her to come out and hang for the weekend. She'd said no. Maybe that was the wrong decision. Of course, Julia insisting she had a ton of details to share about Tom had been an incentive not to go. She hadn't quite brought herself to delete him from her social media, but she had at least unfollowed him. Now she had to seek out his pages to see what was going on, and that urge got weaker with each passing day. When had she last looked? Tuesday?

"No." Claire frowned. "Well, maybe. But Danny will probably show up. He can't say no to pizza. So three couples and three fifth wheels. That's better odds than usual."

"Except if I wasn't here, then you and Danny could pair up and there'd just be four couples." Like there usually were, right?

Claire snorted. "No chance of that. In fact, if you're up for a rebound relationship, I'm guessing Danny'd be good with it. He'll hit on you at least twice tonight. He can't seem to help himself."

"He's a player, then? No, thank you." Larissa had had enough of that sort with Tom. Charming. Friendly. Butter wouldn't melt. "And I hope you're not holding out for him. Guys like that will get you to upend your entire life until everything you do revolves around them and then drop you in the mud."

"Who are we talking about?" Deidre flopped into a chair on the other side of Claire. "Jeremiah got an emergency call— busted septic line—so he's not going to make it."

"Poor guy. But that ups the potential for a movie that's not about racking up a body count." Claire nudged her sister with her elbow.

Deidre grinned. "That is a positive. Who're we trashing? Anyone I know?"

"I think maybe Larissa's ex. We started with Danny, but I get the feeling we veered off." Claire cast Larissa an enquiring glance.

"Sorta. It sounds like Danny's cut from the same pattern." Larissa shrugged. "Aren't all men?"

"Nope." Deidre reached across the table and laid her hand briefly on Larissa's. "I can't fathom how you feel after what Tom did to you. He's a world class idiot. But there are good men out there. In fact, I lean toward thinking the majority of them are."

Were they? "Maybe. The taken ones, at least."

Claire and Deidre exchanged a look before Claire spoke. "Should we get Duncan, Matt and Danny to go help Jeremiah? Make it a girls' night?"

"You don't need to do that. I'm not great company. I think I'll spend the night up in my room and not poison everyone else's evening." Larissa scooted her chair back and would have stood, if Claire's hand hadn't clamped onto her arm.

"Stop that. You're not poisoning anything. Have you talked to anyone about what happened?" Claire frowned. "I don't mean like a shrink—not that that's a bad thing necessarily—but your friends?"

Larissa snorted. "What friends? Look, the farther I get from the wedding, the more I'm realizing how much I let Tom shape my life. I had friends when we met. He didn't like them. Or they didn't like him. So it was easy enough to get too busy to pursue anything. Tom had friends, and they were welcoming. When it all boils down? I don't think I can handle eating the quantity of crow required to get my friends back."

"I suspect you're underestimating your friends, but I'll let it go." Deidre tipped back in her chair, balancing neatly on the rear legs. "That's not really rearranging your whole life. Friendships are bound to have to adjust one way or another when you're serious about someone. Marriage is a process of merging two separate lives into coordinating ones."

Larissa's shoulders drooped. Tom had always emphasized the two becoming one aspect of things. Of course, he'd only meant her life bowing to his. "That's just where it started. I'd been planning to teach abroad. It's been something I've wanted to do for as long as I can remember. That plan fed my education —all the choices I made—right up until I met Tom. Now, instead of teaching at a private school with one or two adjunct courses at the community college, I teach solely online. Tom was sure I needed more flexibility in my schedule, and pay wasn't an issue since he makes good money. Now I scrape by, but affording a good apartment in Richmond is a pipe dream. Yes, I'm on some waiting lists, but even if something opens up, I'm not sure I can accept."

"So go teach overseas!"

"Claire." Deidre nudged her sister in the ribs. "It's probably not that simple."

Larissa blinked. It couldn't be that easy. Could it? "I—huh. It never even occurred to me."

"It's been what? Three weeks? I don't think you're supposed to have your life completely back together three weeks after something like that." Claire shrugged. "Maybe I'm wrong."

"She's not wrong." Deidre tipped forward and bounced to her feet. "I hear a truck. Probably Azure and Matt with the food."

Larissa watched Deidre leave. The woman was full of energy —the impression of constant motion emphasized by how small she was. She looked back at Claire. "Thanks."

"For what?"

"Pointing out the obvious?"

Claire laughed. "I'm told I'm good at that. I do tend to agree with Dee—you're three weeks out from trauma, so you're not supposed to have all the answers and a fix in place yet. Friends? We're good at helping you get there. I'm a little surprised, actually, that you haven't talked to Sean."

"Sean? Why would I?" Larissa furrowed her brow. Sean was nice. And sure, they were friends of a sort. "He's not really the kind of guy you go to when you need to fix your life."

"Hmm. I'll admit I don't know him as well as Anna—or even Dee—but I'd say that's exactly the kind of guy he is. Plus, he likes you."

"Likes me? He likes everybody." Larissa turned as the scent of pizza hit her. Matt and Azure, along with Deidre, Anna, and Duncan charged into the room, talking loudly.

Claire leaned closer, her eyes sparkling. "Keep telling yourself that."

Larissa blinked. Stunned. Sean? No. Claire was out of her mind. He was nice and had paid attention to her first because she was his client, then because they became sort-of-friends. Now? He probably felt sorry for her. And needed to make sure she wasn't going to leave nasty reviews of his business online. She winced. No. That wasn't him at all. She could probably trash him on all sorts of social media and he'd just apologize to her. She sighed and dragged her attention back to the Friday night crowd gathering around the table.

It was time to put on a cheerful face and fit in. Later, she'd dig around on her laptop and get out her overseas teaching plans. What would she need to do to put that back into motion? She was free of Tom. It was time to start acting like it.

9

Sean slid into an empty booth in the bar area of the small chain restaurant. His feet nearly sang with relief. What a long, crazy day. At least the rehearsal was over. If his usual process held true, the sheer number of emergencies he'd managed today would mean a smooth wedding tomorrow. Please, God, let that be the case. Right now, everything on his schedule was wedding-related, but he had some church events coming up when school got out and he would have to carve out time to start on those soon. While still keeping brides from turning into monsters and still juggling a hundred little details that took on inflated importance for the couple planning to tie the knot.

That was the job. He loved every minute of it. When he didn't hate it.

"What can I get you?" The server snapped her gum before glancing over her shoulder and hollering, "I'll be right there."

"Busy tonight. I'll do the mushroom swiss burger, medium, with fries."

"And to drink? We have some great local brews on tap plus—"

"Just water. With a lime?"

"Sure, hon." The little enthusiasm she'd had when she first greeted him was now completely gone. She spun and hurried to a table packed with guys wearing matching baseball jerseys.

Sean leaned back and let his gaze drift between the six TVs. They all had sports of one variety or another on, but it still beat cooking and having to clean up at home. A man slid past, neck craning. He looked familiar. The guy turned and Sean lifted his fingers in greeting. "Hey, man."

Topher blinked. "Sean. Hey. Can I join you? There's a crazy wait for a regular table, so they said check the bar. But it's slammed in here, too."

Sean gestured to the other side of the booth. "Sure. You're not working an event tonight?"

"No, thank goodness. I've got the Masterson-Brinks wedding tomorrow. That's not one of yours."

"Nope. From what I hear, that's a good thing. Although my wedding tomorrow is going to have its own set of issues. They've got four type 1 diabetics in the wedding party, and of course it's in the evening and dinner isn't until after. I'm aiming for plates to be served at eight. Sharp. Each of the diabetics insists they'll be fine, but I've stashed candy and juice boxes everywhere I can think of."

Topher laughed. "That could be interesting. How'd you miss the Masterson wedding?"

"They didn't reach out to me until November. I was already booked. When did they get you?"

"About then. Guess I'm not as popular as you are."

"Please." Sean leaned back as the server brought his water.

She frowned at Topher. "Are you eating?"

"I'd like to." Topher raised his eyebrows at Sean before rattling off his order. The server huffed away. "She's friendly."

"Started out better, but I didn't order a beer. If you don't start with alcohol, you're not going to keep on getting more alcohol, which means the tab is lower and, thus, the tip." Sean shrugged. "I get it. She doesn't know I'm a good tipper."

"I usually am. Not sure that's going to be the case tonight. Never really appreciate being made to feel like an inconvenience when it's her job."

"Come on, man, you know what the service industry is like. She's probably having a bad day. Give her some grace."

"Yeah, yeah." Topher drummed his fingers on the table. "Can I ask you a hypothetical?"

What would it be this time? Topher was the king of random situations. Sean always enjoyed trying to pick through what was reality and what was his friend's desperate imagination. "Sure."

"Would you do a gay wedding?"

Sean's eyebrows shot up. "I—I've never thought about it. Most of my wedding business comes from church. Friends of friends. That kind of thing."

"That's what this would be. If you're willing to consider it."

"You've got a more diverse circle than I realized."

Topher's laugh held no mirth. "Not really. Brian is a holdover from grade school. But he and Dave are good guys."

Sean nodded. It seemed like the safest response. It wasn't that gay people couldn't be good—that was ridiculous. They were people, the same as anyone, with a mix of good, bad, and in-between. Sometimes depending on the day. Or the hour of the day. "Are they Christians?"

"Gosh, no." Topher waited while the server set his soda in front of him and assured them their food should be right out. He sighed. "No. Brian wants nothing to do with Jesus or the church. Never has. His parents might have grown up in the church— they have that built-in 'be a good person and it'll work out' thing going on. Why?"

"I don't know. I guess it matters, a little. I mean, I try not to do weddings for couples who are already living together, although I can't say I've never done it. I do make it clear I believe they're living in sin. Mostly they laugh and call me old fashioned." Sean spun his water glass. "At the end of the day, I figure getting married helps them stop choosing a sinful lifestyle, at least in that regard. But that wouldn't be the same for a gay couple."

"True. But does it matter if they're not professing Christ?"

"That's a question. Maybe it doesn't. I mean, why would people who don't love Jesus live like He told us to? Especially when half the time, His followers don't, either. Myself included. Sin's sin, right? I certainly haven't achieved perfection."

"That's not what I hear."

"What do you mean?"

Topher grinned like a scheming cat. "There's a certain florist who seems to believe you spend your spare time walking across lakes without getting wet."

Sean cringed. "Vanessa."

"Got it in one." Topher chuckled. "I take it the feeling isn't mutual?"

"Dude. It's so far from mutual. Have you heard her giggle?"

"I'm not sure I have. In fact, I'm almost convinced she's permanently PMSing."

"She's not that bad."

"You're not working with her the same way I have to. I've made the mistake of touching her flowers before. That wedding at Peacock Hill? That was mild."

Was this where Sean suggested maybe his friend not move her flowers? How hard was it to talk to her about problems instead of taking things into his own hands? He studied Topher and reached for his water. "You could always try not moving her flowers."

Topher rolled his eyes. "Then it's just something else. At

least if I move her flowers, she blows up, the problem gets solved, and she leaves me alone for the rest of the event."

"Wait. You're doing it on purpose? That's uncool."

Topher shrugged.

Sean bit his tongue as their food was delivered. "You want to bless the meal?"

"I guess." Topher bowed his head and rattled off a quick prayer before picking up his fork and twirling it in his alfredo. "So. Can I give your name to Brian?"

Right. Vanessa sidetracked that conversation. Sean picked up his burger and took a huge bite, stalling for time. What was the right thing? They needed Jesus. That much was obvious—everyone who didn't have Jesus needed Him. Could he shine a little light into their lives if he helped them? On the flip side, if he did help them, was he somehow complicit in their sin? He swallowed. The food went down like a solid lump. "Yeah, I guess."

"Cool." Topher reached for his soda. "So what about you and Vanessa?"

"There is no me and Vanessa. She's a florist I use sometimes." When there's absolutely nobody else available. But that didn't need to be said. Topher clearly had his own negative opinion of the woman, and Sean wasn't going to add to it. She was nice. When she wanted to be. "That's it."

"Uh huh. Nobody special in your life right now?"

Larissa. She was special. But there was no way he was telling Topher about her. Especially when there was virtually no chance of anything ever happening between Larissa and him. "Nope. What about you?"

HE HAD LOST HIS MIND. That was the only possible explanation for why he was pulling off the highway and driving up the winding road leading to Peacock Hill. Oh, he had excuses ready. He had several church groups interested in booking retreats here, but he could have called. Or emailed. On a work day, instead of Sunday after church.

For all he knew, Larissa wasn't even there.

It would serve him right.

He stopped at the bottom of the gravel road that served as a driveway and lowered his head to the steering wheel. He was pathetic. And obvious. None of that changed anything. He still wanted to be here. Even if he only got to see her in passing, he'd know she was okay. If Sunday was meant to be a day of rest, didn't it make sense to do what he could to ease his mind?

Sean snorted. That was some impressive justification, even to his own ears.

A horn beeped.

He flicked his gaze into the rearview mirror and shook his head. Great. He eased toward the house, going slow to try and minimize the gravel dings on his car. After parking, he grabbed his backpack and waited by the front steps while Matt and Azure hopped out of her classic pickup.

"Did we have an appointment I forgot about?" Azure dug through the tiny leather purse draped diagonally across her torso. The long fringe hanging off the bag somehow managed to coordinate with the riot of colors in her ankle-length, gypsy-like skirt. She certainly had a style of her own.

"I don't think he's here for us." Matt shot Sean a grin. "Am I right?"

Sean dug for his dignity. "I need to talk to Claire about some potential bookings."

"Uh-huh." Matt crossed to the steps and gave Sean's arm a light punch. "Sure you do. You eat yet?"

It was almost two in the afternoon. Were there people who

managed to skip eating that long? "Yeah. I hit a drive-through after church. You haven't eaten?"

"We did. Jeremiah's mom invited everyone over after church to see the water feature Jeremiah and Duncan just finished in the backyard. Have to admit it's pretty cool. And his dad's always looking for a reason to fire up the grill. They should all be getting back shortly. Why don't you come on in?" Matt took the stairs two at a time.

Azure breezed by Sean, still rummaging through her tiny purse. "Come on. I have a key in here somewhere."

"Deidre finally started locking up?" Sean followed Azure up the stairs. "Smart."

"Yeah. If we have an event or a group staying, then we leave things open and everyone just locks their individual spaces, but she figured with the TVs and computers we have now it was worth doing. Aha." Azure tugged a key from the bag and handed it to Matt.

Matt unlocked the door and pushed it open before handing the key back to Azure. "Since Claire's not here yet, is there anything we need to do for our wedding?"

Sean couldn't stop the stab of longing as Matt and Azure exchanged a gooey look. Not every couple hit him the same way, but the folks at Peacock Hill were special. All of them. "Probably. We can sit somewhere, and I'll get out my book and take a look."

"Dining room or lounge?"

"Lounge." Azure started in that direction. "Those chairs Jeremiah made are pretty, but they're not comfortable for very long. And if you tell him I said that, I'll murder you in your sleep."

"I'm terrified." Matt shook his head. "She wants people to think she has a mean streak, but I don't think anyone buys it."

"Just wait, Matt Patterson. Just you wait." Azure burrowed into the corner of a couch and tucked her feet up under her.

Matt snuggled in beside her and kissed her cheek. "As long as it's not too much longer."

Sean cleared his throat. "I can go in another room for a while, if you want."

Azure laughed and shoved at Matt's shoulder. "Scoot. You're making him uncomfortable and I don't want to get stuck planning our wedding. You leave it up to me, and we'll be hitting the courthouse and that barbecue restaurant over in Waynesboro and calling it a day."

"And my aunt would never speak to either of us again. Which . . . no. No. As fantastic as that sounds sometimes, I couldn't do that to Uncle Jim." Matt turned laughing eyes to Sean. "How's that planning going?"

Sean scanned the pages in his book dedicated to Matt and Azure's upcoming Labor Day weekend wedding. "Azure still needs a dress."

She groaned.

"I promise it's not going to be that bad. You just need to pick a day to meet me in either Charlottesville or Richmond, and we'll get it squared away."

"Can't I just find something online? Dress shopping sounds like torture."

"What if Matt came along?"

Matt frowned. "I—no. Wedding dress shopping? No. Why would I?"

"You're Christians. You don't seriously believe it's bad luck for you to see her dress beforehand, right?" How many times had Sean had some variation of this conversation with couples he was helping? He should start charging for psychiatric services, like that girl in the old cartoon with the round-headed kid.

Matt nodded slowly.

"Okay. So, since seeing her dress prior to the wedding isn't going to cause some bizarre doom to your marriage, and the woman you're marrying is scared to do it by herself—"

"I'm not scared." Azure crossed her arms and glowered at Sean. "Hesitant. I'll go with hesitant."

Sean lifted his hands. "Sorry." He pinned Matt with a look. "With a *hesitant* bride-to-be, I know I'd want to do anything I could to try and help. Even if it meant braving a bridal shop or two."

Matt scrubbed his hands over his face. "Yeah, fine. We can close the garage and go. Choose a day."

"We don't have to close." Azure drummed her fingers on her leg. "Uncle Jim's in town right now, and we have Melvin. Maybe he could come in a full day instead of half? They should be able to handle anything that needs doing for one day, right?"

"Sure. Of course. And knowing Aunt Ida, she won't want to let my uncle out of her sight, so she'll come in and handle the front desk. Probably spend the whole time researching their next trip." Matt reached for Azure's hand. "Which takes us back to: choose a day, and we'll make it work."

"You're sure?" Azure glanced at Matt, then back to Sean. "What's good for you? And the whole dress thing—why does it feel awkward?"

Sean couldn't stop the chuckle. "Because we're culturally conditioned to think it's bad luck. But there's more flexibility with your schedule if you don't insist on the dress tradition. We can do photos before the ceremony, for example, and not keep everyone waiting before the reception."

"Oh." Azure's eyes lit. "That's a fantastic idea."

"And, if you're worried about capturing that first moment when he sees you in your gown, we can make sure that's part of the photography."

"But I'll have seen her in the gown already. At the shop."

"It's completely different. Trust me." He flipped through his book to stare at the calendar before listing a handful of dates that would work for him. "I think we can probably do Charlottesville rather than Richmond, which will save you some drive time. We should be able to find the right look in one of the shops there. Let me know which of those dates works for you when you talk to everyone about handling the garage."

Matt tapped at his phone with an absentminded nod. "Done. Maybe they'll text back today."

"Jim won't. Your aunt's on her no-electronics-on-Sunday kick, remember?"

Matt snickered. "No. I'd forgotten. She's going to have to get over that before we're back to football season. Uncle Jim can humor her when it's mostly baseball and golf."

"Hey. Did y'all see Sean's car is here?" Claire barreled into the room and stopped with a laugh. "And Sean too, apparently. Wedding stuff?"

"Not really. Killing time until everyone was back." Matt pushed off the couch. "I'm going to go grab a soda. Anyone else want one?"

Azure raised her fingers. Claire shot him a toothy grin and batted her eyelashes.

Sean shrugged. "Why not. Thanks."

Claire perched on the arm of Sean's chair. "What brings you out our way this afternoon? I thought you didn't work on Sundays."

His face heated. Normally, he didn't. "I was hoping we could discuss a couple of potential church retreats for this summer."

"Uh-huh." Claire cocked her head to the side. "That's it?"

Azure rolled her eyes and mock-whispered, "Where's Larissa?"

Claire grinned. "That's what I figured. Deidre has her trapped in the kitchen right now, but she was talking about spending the rest of the day in her room."

"Maybe I'll go see if Matt needs help with the drinks." Sean hurried from the room and ignored—or tried to ignore—the laughter following him. It wasn't as if he'd successfully hidden anything from anyone anyway. Or so it seemed.

Matt pushed open the kitchen door and looked in. Deidre stood with her arms crossed, scowling at Larissa.

"I don't see why you're upset. This has nothing to do with you." Larissa punctuated her words with a stabbing finger in Deidre's direction.

Matt slid along the wall, soda cans in his arm and hissed, "Dude. Run. Save yourself, or you're going to get caught up in this."

"What—" Sean snapped his mouth closed on the question as Matt thrust a soda at him and slipped out of the kitchen. Okay. He eyed the can and, with a shrug, popped the top.

Deidre spun. When her gaze landed on Sean she nodded. "Good. Maybe you can talk some sense into her."

"I—what's—hi. Just got here. A little lost?" Sean took a long drink, but it did nothing to soothe his burning throat.

"Larissa's leaving."

"Leaving?" His gaze flicked to Larissa and he drew his eyebrows together. "You got an apartment already? That's great."

Deidre snorted. "Not hardly. She's—"

"Can I speak for myself? If not, I'll just go and leave you to it." Larissa scooted back her chair in preparation for rising.

"You sit right back down and tell him what you told me." Deidre spun on her heel and pinned Sean with an icy glare. "Talk some sense into her."

He watched her stride from the room. For someone so tiny,

she had a lot of presence. He took another drink and turned back to Larissa. "Um. Hi?"

Larissa pressed her fingers to her eyes. "You might as well sit down if you're going to yell at me."

"I wasn't planning on yelling. What's going on?" He slid onto a stool across from Larissa and spun his soda can in tiny circles.

10

"I'm moving." Larissa looked Sean square in the eye, challenging him to disagree.

"But not into an apartment?"

Why was she explaining herself to everyone? They weren't lifelong friends. They were—what? Acquaintances at best, right? Except Sean. He was a friend. Hadn't she spent an inordinate amount of time thinking about the fact that they were friends? If he was a friend, then he probably deserved an explanation. "Can I have a sip of that?"

Sean slid the can across the table. "I can get you your own."

Larissa took a drink and handed it back. "Wow, that's sweet. I'm good. I always forget what the non-diet stuff tastes like."

"There might be diet in the fridge." Sean started to rise.

"I'm good. Just sit." She pinched the bridge of her nose. Where were all the words? She'd had no trouble explaining—and justifying—her decision to Deidre when the woman backed her into a corner. Now, with Sean, she worried how it was going to come across. "Okay. So you know I'm an English teacher, right?"

He nodded.

"Of course you do. All my life—not hyperbole here, my *entire* life—my dream was to teach English overseas. I got a degree and a special certification that opens doors for teaching English as a second language. Before I met Tom, I taught in a Christian school and as an adjunct at the community college, plus doing the online tutoring and saving every penny so I'd have a good nest egg when I went overseas."

"Seems reasonable. Did you have a timeline?"

See? That was a good question. She nodded. "I was about six months away from leaving when I met Tom. He was not on board with the idea. Travel overseas? Sure. But live there? No way, no how. Most of our big fights had to do with long-term plans, but I thought—hoped—he'd come around. Or we'd figure out a way to compromise. Something. He was important enough to me that I was willing to see how we could meet in the middle."

"Of course you were. You were going to marry the guy. What happened?"

Larissa shook her head. "I don't even know. First it was 'Oh, baby, you work too hard. Why don't you give up one of your jobs? You never have time for me.' So I took a term off the online teaching. But that wasn't enough. After all, he made plenty of money, and we could start a family as soon as I wanted, and before I knew it, I'd quit as an adjunct and put in my resignation at the school. But I'm not cut out for sitting around the house all day—I had to do something. So I picked up the online tutoring again—more students than I had before, but I made sure I was completely done by the time he finished work so he couldn't say it interfered with our time together. And now, here we are. I'm seriously underemployed and stuck in a city that was fine for a temporary spot while I prepped for what I really wanted to do, but isn't the kind of place I want to call home forever."

Sean's eyes shuttered and he picked up his soda but didn't

drink. "So when Deidre said you're moving, she meant overseas."

"Yeah. I've been in touch with a couple of placement agencies. There are a ton of opportunities, and they don't have to be long term. I can hang out for six months, maybe a year, and then move on if I want." She grinned. "Best of all, as long as I'm somewhere there's Internet—which, let's face it, is basically anywhere these days—I can keep doing my online tutoring to supplement my income. Or I can take on private students locally. Or both. As long as I'm managing my time, it doesn't look like it'll matter."

"That's great. Where are you headed? When?"

Larissa frowned. His words were exactly right, but his tone left a lot to be desired. Where was the enthusiasm? "Try not to get too excited."

"Sorry. I—it's not something I saw coming. If it's what you want to do, then you should do it. Totally."

She searched his expression, trying to understand it, then gave up. He was right. It was something she wanted—no, needed —to do. And she was going to. "I'm weighing options. Right now it's between Brazil and the Ukraine."

"Those are completely different."

Larissa laughed. "I know. The best part is, I can choose one and do the other later if that's what I want."

"When will you go?" Sean tipped the last of his soda into his mouth and set the can down with a hollow thunk.

"Mid-May."

"Two weeks. That's fast. Wow."

She shrugged. "Why wait? My stuff is already stored. I'm basically homeless. And I'm four years behind schedule, thanks to Tom."

"Let me know how I can help, okay? Ride to the airport, whatever."

"Right now, all I need to do is figure out where I'm going and get the visa paperwork started. The placement agency says they have special channels for expediting permission, so it shouldn't take as long as they say it can online." She stood and patted his shoulder as she passed him. "But I might take you up on the airport ride if you're serious."

"Of course I am." Sean stood and tossed his can at the recycle bin by the kitchen door. "What will you do with your car?"

That was another wrinkle to iron out. It wasn't old. It still worked great. She should sell it and add the proceeds to her bank account. All the online calculators indicated she should be able to support herself with her salary from teaching English, but if her engagement to Tom had taught her anything, it was that life didn't always go to plan. Following Sean, she pushed through the kitchen door and headed toward the stairs.

After a glance at the magnificent stained glass window dominating the staircase landing, she paused on the first step and turned. "I don't know yet. It's on my list of things to figure out."

"If you decide to keep it, I have an extra parking spot at my place. I can even drive it for you now and then."

"Why are you helping me so much?" Larissa frowned. "We aren't best friends. We barely know each other beyond planning for a wedding that never happened. I don't understand why any of this should matter to you."

Sean stared at her for the space of two heartbeats before closing the distance between them. He put his hands on her shoulders and drew her close as his mouth descended to hers. For one moment, she froze, then her hands slid around his neck, her eyes drifted shut, and she lost herself in the magic of his kiss.

Much too quickly, Sean stepped back. "I hope that answers your question."

Larissa gaped as he turned on his heel and strode through the foyer and out the front door. She forced herself to take a deep breath. And then another. She touched her lips with the tips of her fingers and sank to the step. She'd just rest here until her knees weren't too weak to carry her upstairs.

AT FOUR IN THE MORNING, Larissa finally gave up on sleeping. She tossed on clothes, pulled her hair into a messy knot on the back of her head and stared at herself in the mirror. She should go ahead and shower. Do her makeup. Make herself presentable. But what was the point? Her students didn't care what she looked like, and there was no one at Peacock Hill to impress. Sean . . . unbidden, her fingers moved to cover her lips. What had he been thinking?

She turned away from the mirror and grabbed her Bible and the little spiral notebook she kept with it. In theory, writing her prayers should help her focus and listen. Like a lot of her spiritual life, she wasn't convinced it worked, but she wasn't going to give up on it just yet. At least she was going to try not to. Maybe it didn't work for the same reasons Tom left. She was unlovable.

Someone ought to tell Sean.

Larissa rolled her eyes as she crept down the stairs. Her gaze flicked to the stained glass peacock as she passed. Bet that bird had seen it all. *He hoped it answered her question.* Too bad the bird couldn't talk. Sean's kiss hadn't answered any of her questions. It had only raised more. And those queries had kept her tossing around all night long.

Larissa paused at the bottom of the stairs and bit her lip. She could detour to the kitchen, make some coffee, sit at the table, and pretend there was going to be something relevant to her in whatever fantastic Old Testament chapter was next in her Bible reading plan. Or there was that bench by the lake she'd seen when she was tramping around the grounds. She turned to look back up at the dark window. Not even the sun was up yet. That ruled out trying to find the bench. The way her life was going, she'd wander straight into the water or step on a snake. Maybe both.

She headed toward the kitchen but stopped with her hand on the swinging door. She didn't need coffee, and coffee was the first thing anyone else who got up early would come looking for. Did Deidre and Jeremiah have their own little kitchen in their basement apartment? Probably. She couldn't remember. Same with Claire. With Anna and Duncan out in the cottage, maybe no one would come in here and find her. She wrinkled her nose and padded past. She'd try something new.

Deidre had called it the breakfast room when she'd given Larissa her tour. Paintings of birds and ivy wound around the walls. It had a fanciful effect that blended well with the potted plants and floor-to-ceiling window looking out over one of the sunken gardens. In the center of the room was a glass-topped oval table surrounded by six padded wicker chairs.

Larissa switched on the chandelier and settled in one of the seats, angling herself so she could look out the window into the shadowy darkness beyond. She glanced at her Bible before setting it aside and, instead, opened her notebook. She paged through, shaking her head at the ridiculous optimism in her prayers leading up to the wedding. She'd prayed for good weather—and God had delivered. She couldn't say otherwise. Apparently, she'd neglected to pray that Tom would show up.

They'd be coming up on a month of marriage if he had. Two weeks of honeymoon. Two weeks of normal life. Would it still be exciting and new? It would have to be, wouldn't it? Shouldn't she still be heartbroken that they weren't? Instead, she was . . . what? Relieved. It was the one word that wouldn't go away. Sean's kiss had only amplified the feeling.

Who knew kisses could be like that?

Kissing Tom had been pleasant, but had never left her noodle-kneed.

She'd tried to talk to her mom about it. Once. Mom had gone on and on about unrealistic expectations set by popular culture, romance novels in particular. After all, no one was as good-looking in real life as those people on the covers of books. Not even the people on the covers of the books. Those were models, with hair and makeup and photo-editing software at their disposal. The conversation had left Larissa steadier, if a little disillusioned. But if people in real life didn't share electrifying, pulse-racing kisses, she'd determined to be satisfied with pleasant. And maybe, like Mom had suggested, it would get better with time.

Sean's kiss had shattered that notion.

She could have—would have—been satisfied kissing Tom for the rest of her life. Now? She didn't know how she'd be satisfied kissing anyone other than Sean.

11

"Hey, Matt." Sean reached for his friend's hand and shook it, clapping his shoulder with his other hand. "Azure. You look nice."

Azure glanced down and shrugged. "Didn't feel like overalls was the right look for this."

Sean chuckled. "It would've been fine. I'm surprised you could get the garage covered so quickly."

"Uncle Jim's going stir-crazy at home with Aunt Ida. He jumped at the chance, although I did hear my aunt promising to come by with lunch and stay for the afternoon." Matt shook his head. "She loves having him around. I'm hoping they'll figure out their retirement dynamic sooner rather than later."

"I'm sure they will. Ida will wear down your uncle until he's content spending every minute of every day in the same room with her. I think the company is all she's after. He doesn't have to actively participate in whatever she's doing. At least that's my read." Azure nodded toward the bridal salon. "We're going in here?"

"We are. I made us an appointment." Sean had called in two different favors to get it, but that wasn't worth mentioning.

What was the point of earning favors if they never got used? "But don't stress if we aren't successful here. I have two more places to try."

"Do we have appointments there, too?"

Sean shook his head. He'd learned that lesson early in his wedding planning career. Make one appointment for the morning and schedule the more flexible shops for the afternoon. The key was to know the client and merchandise. And he did. It would be a bit of a shock if Azure didn't find exactly what she was looking for here. "Shouldn't need them."

She chewed her lower lip. "I really want to get this handled today."

Sean patted her shoulder. "Stop worrying and trust me. Let's go."

Matt dragged the door open and wrinkled his nose. "Are you sure—?"

"Yes." Sean nudged Matt inside and held the door for Azure. The quiet strains of harp music drifted through the air and the faint scent of vanilla permeated each breath. It was very feminine. Sean's brides always loved it. He hadn't brought many grooms, but he imagined Matt was mentally rolling his eyes. The same way Sean was. Still, a shop that catered to women was bound to be overtly female. He'd gotten used to it.

"Hello? Can I help—oh, Sean." The woman beamed and crossed the room with both hands out. When she was near, she clasped both of his hands and made air kisses on each of his cheeks. "You're right on time, as always. This must be your bride?"

"Azure, this is Simone. Simone, Azure. And her fiancé, Matt."

Simone shook each hand, shooting a surreptitious look at Sean as he introduced Matt. "How lovely and modern. We get a lot of moms, not so many grooms."

"My mom's in Arizona. I—Sean was positive it was okay."

Azure's face was bright pink and she shot a pleading glance at Sean.

"Of course it is. Right, Simone?"

"Oh yes, yes. It's just unusual." Simone patted Azure's hand. "I pulled a few ideas based on what Sean said when he set up the appointment. Why don't we go back and start with those? If they don't suit, we'll look around some more. Sean, I set up the larger space for you since we're not busy this morning."

They weren't busy? Then why had Simone insisted she was doing him a favor by getting them on the schedule? Whatever. "Okay. We'll wait there."

Sean led Matt to the seating area and gestured to the arc of stuffed chairs.

"Fancy." Matt settled in one of the pink seats and glanced around. "It's girly. You know Azure isn't, right?"

Sean laughed. "I know that. I told Simone. But I also think this is the most likely place to find something unique—which is what I think Azure wants."

"She doesn't know what she wants. Every time she tries to look at dresses she flips three pages before she wings the magazine across the room. Honestly? I'd be happy if she gave up and decided to wear her overalls. I bet she could paint something fun and weddingish on them and we could go with it."

That would be very Azure. Maybe not so wedding. "It's a fallback position."

"You're humoring the fish out of water. I get it." Matt shifted in his seat. "How long does it take to try on a dress?"

"Man, you have no idea. You want a drink? They have bottled water and sodas—usually Simone offers, but I guess she was excited to show Azure the dresses she pulled."

"Nah. I'm good. Just—are you sure it's okay for me to be here?"

Again? Hadn't they had this conversation? Sean opened his

mouth to launch into his explanation one more time, when Simone appeared in his peripheral vision.

Simone paused, bouncing slightly on the balls of her feet. Sean fought a grin. That was her tell that she, at least, loved the dress. "Are you two ready?"

Matt straightened.

"Absolutely."

"Come on out, Azure. Let's show this off." Simone held out a hand.

Several heartbeats ticked past before Azure appeared, her hands pressed to her belly. A white skirt billowed around her legs, but it was the tiny pops of color at her waist, trailing up the bodice that caught the eye. Sean nodded. It was perfect.

Matt blinked and drew in a breath.

"What? Is that bad?" Azure turned and held Matt's gaze.

"No. You look amazing. I've never seen a wedding dress with —are those flowers? The color is amazing. Is it okay?"

"There aren't rules, really. It's your wedding." Simone helped Azure onto the round platform in front of a three-paneled mirror. "Sean mentioned that Azure was an artist and not afraid to be quirky. So I started with less conventional dresses. This fits like it was made for her. What do you think, Azure?"

"It's . . ." Azure ran her hands down her hips and a slow smile spread across her face. "Why aren't dresses like this in the magazines?"

Simone's laugh tinkled out. "They are. Not usually at the front, though. You have to look through the mass of the usual before you find them. Most brides—even those who say they're non-traditional—want something that leans traditional. And we can go that route, if you decide you'd like to."

Azure's head started shaking before Simone finished speaking.

Matt chuckled.

Azure looked over her shoulder. "What do you think, Matt?"

"You look amazing. It's a gorgeous dress. And it's you."

"Sean?" Azure's gaze darted to him.

Sean stood and came closer, pausing to fluff the short train as he walked in a circle around Azure. It was better than he'd imagined. And that was the reason Simone was always his first stop when he had a bride who wanted something other than what could be found in any bridal department. "I love it. I was a bit worried the skirt might be too full, but it's good. You can carry it. What's your feeling?"

"I love it. I—I can't choose my first dress, can I?"

Simone laughed. "Of course you can. But we can try on another, if you want to be sure."

That was a risk. Sean had followed brides through what felt like hundreds of shops, only to end up with the first dress. "Could I see what else you pulled?"

Simone sent him a knowing smile and nodded. "Of course. You wait here, Azure, and I'll be right back."

He followed Simone, catching a glimpse of Matt moving to stand beside Azure as they turned down the hall to the dressing rooms.

"You said colorful, and the links to the designers who were starting to incorporate embroidered flowers was a big help," Simone said. "The one she has on is actually one of the dresses you linked."

"I wondered. That's in her budget?" He'd sent specific numbers along as well, and it wasn't like Simone to go outside those. There were other bridal consultants who were all about trying to get people to ignore their limitations. Simone had never been like that. It was another reason he went to her.

"Just. And I have a little flex with how I can apply a discount or two to make sure tax doesn't push us over." Simone beamed at him. "I don't do that for just anyone, you realize."

"You're the best." She was also married—point three in her favor—so he didn't consider this flirting. His gaze darted to her left hand and the enormous rock that still sparkled from the proper digit.

Simone's laugh rang out, filling the dressing room. "I wasn't coming on to you, I promise."

Sean's face heated. Busted.

She unhooked a simpler gown from the back of the door. "If she's going to try something else on, I'd recommend this. It's more traditional—still embroidered, but in the same white so it's much less obtrusive. The style is different as well—more A-line than ballgown. I don't think she should try mermaid."

"I don't think anyone should try mermaid, but they always want to."

Simone laughed again. "Not if they come to me, they don't."

It was true. Another point for Simone. He eyed the dress and nodded. "Good choice. It'll give her a feel. Maybe you can find a way to mention that mermaid isn't a good idea."

"I'll see what I can do. Azure doesn't strike me as someone who's going to lean that way, but I've been surprised before." Simone made a little shooing motion. "Send her back and we'll be just a few minutes."

He left the dressing room and headed back to the seating area, stopping as he turned the corner and spied Matt and Azure wrapped in a kiss. Sean cleared his throat and they broke apart, blushing.

"Practicing for after the pastor says you're husband and wife?" Sean grinned. Hopefully it was clear he was kidding. They weren't the first couple he'd found kissing. As far as he was concerned, kissing your fiancé was a good thing.

"Told you." Matt pecked Azure's cheek and returned to his seat.

"Head on back. Simone has something different for you to try. It should help you decide if you need to keep looking."

Azure stroked the skirt of the dress and bit her lip. "Maybe I should stop? I love this."

"You might love something else more." Matt shrugged.

"Sean?"

Sean tried not to sigh. "Your first instinct was to try something else to be sure. Let's stick with that."

"All right." Azure gathered up her dress and stepped down from the raised platform. "Don't leave."

"Where would we go?" Matt winked at her and settled back in his chair. "Go."

"Not as bad as you expected?" Sean reclaimed his seat next to Matt and prayed Azure's choice would be clear after trying the second gown. He'd cleared the day to work with them, but even as much as he loved all things wedding, dress shopping could be tedious.

"Not so far. I will point out you let Anna shop online."

"We had two weeks to plan, and Anna is not nearly as self-aware as Azure. But if you tell her I said that, I'll call you a filthy liar."

Matt snickered. "Fair enough. I get what you mean. They seem happy in the little cottage. It's nice that they're not trying to make rooms on the third floor work for them. That was their original thought, and I never did see how that would work."

"Have you figured out where you'll live? Neither of you are as tied to Peacock Hill as the rest of the gang. Will Azure move in with you?"

"Over my aunt and uncle's garage? No, thank you. I love them, but I don't need Aunt Ida popping by to see how we're doing whenever she gets a wild hair." Matt glanced in the direction of the fitting rooms and lowered his voice. "I was thinking of talking to Jeremiah about his place."

Sean drew his eyebrows together. "The basement apartment he and Deidre have?"

"No, no. He has a house in town. It's sitting empty since they got married because he hasn't finished all the renovations he wanted to do yet. I thought he might be interested in renting—or selling—to someone he knew would not only let him keep working on it in his spare time, but would take good care of it."

"Nice. Think he'll go for selling?"

"Honestly? I have no idea. I'm not even sure if I'll be able to meet his asking price, but I want to find out." Matt blew out a breath and shifted. "But I should probably ask Azure about it first, right? You don't surprise someone with a house."

Sean snorted out a laugh. "No. No you don't. Talk to Azure. Better yet? See if you can find a way for her to get inside and see it."

"Ready, gentlemen?" Simone poked her head around the corner, eyebrows lifted.

"Absolutely." Sean turned so he could watch Azure cross to the mirrors. The more traditional dress was fine—still bridal, but it lacked the pop of the first dress. Anyone would look lovely in it, but they'd look like every other bride. Azure wasn't every other bride.

Azure stepped onto the raised circle and frowned into the mirrors. "Why don't I love this? It's gorgeous. It's exactly what the magazines are full of—maybe a little different with the embroidered flowers, but still close. Yet it's—"

"Blah. The word you're looking for is blah." Matt stood and circled his bride-to-be. "It's not you, hon. The other dress was."

Sean nodded. "You're both right. It's a lovely dress and I actually think I have a bride it's going to be amazing for. Can you tag it for me and put it in the back, Simone? I'll see if I can get her out here this week."

"Of course. Assuming Azure doesn't want it." Simone made a

few small adjustments to the dress before standing to Azure's side and tilting her head. "You do look quite pretty in it."

"Thanks. I—no. I want the other dress." Azure gave a determined nod. "That's the one."

"Do you want to try it on again to be sure? Then we could look at headpieces and shoes as well." Simone pressed her lips together. "How were you thinking you'd wear your hair? There's so much of it."

"Headpieces? Like a veil? I don't want a veil. I thought I'd braid it into a crown like I sometimes do and add some flowers. Is that okay?" Azure tugged her long braid and wrapped it around her head to demonstrate.

"Of course it is." Simone patted Azure's hand. "You're the bride. And that's flattering on you. I have just the thing to try— why don't you go change back into your regular clothes and I'll be right there."

"You're not going to make me shop for shoes, right?" Matt tucked his hands in his pockets, his shoulders slumping. "I hate shoe shopping."

"I saw a couple of pairs I want her to try before we go, but if they're not right she can go online and figure it out." Sean glanced at Simone. "Is it okay if I grab the shoes while you get whatever you're plotting?"

"Of course. It's not a plot. We just got some gorgeous hairpins with multicolored crystal flowers on the end. I thought they might be a fun accent with a little extra oomph. I'll be right back."

"You want to pull shoes with me?"

Matt shook his head and dropped back into his seat. "I'm good."

Laughing, Sean headed to the front of the store where the shoe display had caught his eye. He snagged two pairs the first dress had brought to mind and returned to see Azure perched on Matt's knee while Simone tucked sparkling pins into Azure's hair.

Simone stepped back. "Go look. It's obviously not perfect, but it gives the idea."

"Oh." Azure turned her head one way, then the other before grinning. "I love them. Thank you."

"They'll be great with the dress. Do you like either of these?" Sean put the two pairs of shoes down in front of Azure. "You won't hurt my feelings if you say no."

Both had a low heel—it was hard to get away from that unless a bride chose ballet flats or sneakers, and Sean wasn't a fan of either. Sure, comfort was important on a big day like a wedding, but sometimes it was worth it to suffer a tiny bit.

Azure tapped a pair with a subtle sparkle. "These are fun."

"Try them. Sean has a good eye—those would be great with your dress."

"My dress." Azure brightened and she turned to Matt. "I have a wedding dress. To marry you in."

Matt leaned forward and pressed his lips to hers. "Can't wait."

Sean looked away and fought off the surge of jealousy that tried to claw through his chest. What was Larissa doing today? Had she made progress on her plans to move overseas?

"What do you think?" Azure twisted her foot, letting the light catch the sparkles on the shoes.

"How do they feel?" Sean dragged his thoughts away from Larissa and pasted on a smile.

Azure took a few steps and bounced in them. "Okay, I guess. No pinching, so that's a start. But I have no idea how they'll do when I'm standing an entire day. I don't know how anyone figures that out."

"They'll do a little better than average, but you'll be ready for a foot rub when the night's over. Happily, you'll have someone available to help with that." Simone laughed and waggled her eyebrows.

Matt grinned.

Sean cleared his throat. "So, yes to the shoes?"

"And to the dress. And pins." Azure clapped her hands together like a giddy toddler.

Simone clasped her hands at her waist. "Congratulations. Let's get you checked out. I don't think we need to schedule any alterations, but I'll make a note to check-in closer to the wedding to see if that's changed."

12

Larissa was crossing the foyer when an engine ruptured the quiet of the afternoon. She wasn't sure where everyone went during the day, but Peacock Hill was a reasonably peaceful place to work. She'd branched out of the business center—the chairs down there were not suited for long periods of use—and set up with her laptop in the lounge. No one seemed to mind.

She scooted closer to the door and watched as Azure and Matt climbed out of her vintage pickup, laughing. Matt grabbed a hanging bag from behind the passenger seat. Azure lunged for it, but he held it out of reach, shaking his head. It looked like Azure found her dress. Good for her.

Larissa ignored the pang in her chest. Her dress was now for sale on several online sites. She'd get some of her money back, and some other woman would enjoy a picture-perfect day in a little girl's dream dress. Mom had tried to convince her to keep it and wear it when she did get married. Larissa snorted. Even if that did happen, she wasn't wearing the dress she'd bought to marry Tom to walk down the aisle to someone else. That was just weird.

She pushed away the flicker of Sean's face and refused to think about it.

The door opened, and Azure and Matt's laughter spilled into the foyer.

"Hey. Successful trip, I see. Congrats."

"Thanks. You want to see it?" Azure could power the house on the wattage coming off her smile.

Not really. "Sure. You want to wait until everyone's around? Then you could put it on once, and we could all see."

"That's a great idea."

Matt leaned over and kissed the tip of Azure's nose. "That sounds like girls night in. I'll see if the guys want to hang."

"It's Wednesday. Don't you have youth?" Azure reached for Matt's hand. "Did you need me to help?"

"Nah. We'll manage. I'll rope Jeremiah into helping, then I'll talk him into making nachos after. Even Duncan likes the way Jeremiah makes them, and Duncan's not a nacho guy. Sean planned to hang in Charlottesville a little longer, right?"

Azure nodded.

"Maybe I'll see if he wants to come down, too. I don't get the sense he has a lot of time for hanging out with the guys."

Larissa's mouth went dry. Sean. She aimed for casual when she spoke. "You'll do the food in the kitchen here? Girls like to eat too, you know."

"Maybe. Or we can see if Jer wants to hang at his house. That way we're not in the way." Matt shrugged.

Right. Jeremiah still owned a house. That had been mentioned . . . . The group had too many conversations and had absorbed her into them, like she was one of them. On one hand, it was nice. On the other? It wasn't something she was used to. Her friends—could she even call them that?—would never have welcomed a stranger like these people did. Heck, they hardly welcomed Tom, and Larissa had been engaged to him. Tom's friends had been a bit more open. But they'd smirked. A lot. Maybe that should have been a clue something was off.

"Okay. Well, keep me posted. I should get back to work—I was taking a quick break when I heard your truck. I'm glad it was a successful trip." Larissa lifted a hand and turned toward the lounge.

Azure and Matt whispered behind her. Larissa ignored it. She didn't need to get involved in their sweet nothings.

"Hey." Azure jogged up. "You okay?"

"Me? Sure."

Azure frowned. "You don't have to see the dress if it's too much. I mean, I don't know if I'd want—after. Ugh. I'm bungling this. I want you to come. But I'll understand if you'd rather not. Just thought I'd make that clear."

"I'm okay. I'd like to see your dress, though I'll admit I'm bummed about the nachos." And not getting a chance to see Sean. Although after that kiss, maybe that was a good thing. She licked her lips. "Please tell me we aren't going to end up with celery or something stupid like that."

Azure swiped a finger across her heart in an X. "Deidre's learned a lot of Jeremiah's nacho tricks. I'll tell her we want real food. Seven?"

"That'll work. Thanks." Larissa settled on the couch and dragged her computer onto her lap. Her email dinged and she checked the time before switching over. A slow grin spread over her face as she scanned the text. Sao Paolo, here she came.

"Dress first. Then food."

"Wait, what? Why?" Azure's voice held the tiniest hint of a whine. "I'm hungry. We should eat first, right Larissa?"

Larissa held up her hands and shook her head. "I'm just here to observe. And eat."

"Aha! Eat. 'Cause you're hungry." Azure frowned at Deidre. "We're *all* hungry."

"Well, the nachos aren't ready yet, so go put your dress on."

Claire snorted. "And that, ladies, is why I gave up trying to win an argument with my sister. You might as well do what she says, Az. She's bossy."

"They're called leadership skills, thank you very much." Deidre crossed her arms and dropped into one of the over-stuffed chairs in the lounge on the main floor of Peacock Hill.

Larissa hadn't realized their girls' night would take place in here. She'd been working away when everyone started to trickle in. Still, it was easy enough to pack up her laptop and put on a smile. Especially now that she had an official countdown. Three weeks. The short timeline put a tiny hitch in her chest just under her heart, but it wasn't as if she had that much to do. Pack, and, well, pack.

"How's work? I noticed you moved up here. The business center is awful, right?" Anna curled up on the other end of the couch Larissa was sitting on. "I don't do any landscape design down there unless I have no other option. Honestly, sitting at the dining room table is better than those chairs. Deidre thinks they're good enough for guests."

"They probably are. I mean, what do guests at a place like this need to do online? Maybe print a boarding pass or check email real fast? It's not like you want them going down there to plug in instead of whatever retreat-y stuff they're supposed to be doing. Right?" Larissa shrugged. She had no idea what sorts of things visitors to Peacock Hill were going to do. She wasn't convinced anyone other than Claire did know.

Claire pointed a finger at Larissa. "Exactly. I happen to agree with Dee about the chairs. They're fine. People who aren't living here shouldn't be down there for long. It's a convenience, not a necessity."

"I guess we'll find out when the first group comes through." Anna puffed out her cheeks and frowned at Claire. "When is that, again?"

Claire tapped at her phone before answering. "End of the month. We have a group coming in for a long weekend over Memorial Day."

"You don't have a wedding booked that weekend? I'm stunned." Thankfully, Larissa would be gone before the retreat season started. Did retreats have a season? Whatever. She'd be gone. That freed up a room and kept her from being in the way. Everybody won.

"I think because we didn't officially open," Claire made air quotes, "for weddings until mid-January everyone who wanted a spring wedding this year was already booked somewhere."

That made sense. Most people, it seemed, started booking venues a year out. Had to, in a lot of cases, because spaces filled fast. Finding Peacock Hill had been a godsend for her, even if it hadn't ended quite the way she wanted. But what if they'd held the wedding at their church and Tom had stood her up in front of everyone she had to see on a weekly basis? Oh, sure, there'd been some folks who had made the trek out, but not on the level that would have happened if they'd had an open invite in the bulletin. She shuddered. One disaster averted at least.

"What about now? Bookings are picking up, right?" Deidre paced between the windows of the room. "You said it was looking good for the spring and summer."

"Chill, Dee, we're fine. We're even starting to get nibbles for weddings next spring. Word's getting out. And we could host about seven different events over Labor Day if we weren't closed for Azure and Matt's wedding." Claire stretched her arms over her head. "I'd tell you if there was an issue."

Deidre opened her mouth to respond but stopped when Azure called out from the hallway.

"You ready?"

"We're ready." Larissa shifted so she could see the doorway.

Azure stepped into view and twisted her fingers together at her waist. "Well?"

"Come stand on the coffee table." Deidre held out a hand. "I want to get the full effect."

"I'm not standing on a coffee table. I'll break it."

"Please. You're tiny. It's sturdy. Get up there." Deidre took Azure's hand and tugged.

Azure shook her head. "That's dumb. Stop. You can see fine."

"Leave her alone, Dee." Anna pulled the coffee table out of the way. "You make me glad I shopped online."

Deidre laughed. "Fine. Whatever. I was trying to make it more like the bridal salon."

"Please. That place was scary. It's so pink. Why was it so pink?" Azure shuddered. "I might have nightmares."

Larissa chuckled. They were all pink. Sean had taken her to four. Maybe five. Who could remember? But they were all pink. "What matters is that you found this gorgeous thing. How many dresses did you try on?"

"Two. But this was the first. I just knew." Azure stroked the skirt. "Is that dumb? They say it on those stupid shows, and I always laughed, but . . ."

"Nope. It's completely different when it's your turn. I get it." Larissa leaned closer to see the delicate and colorful embroidery. "I love the flowers."

"They're so fun, aren't they?" Azure ran a finger along one of the lines of needlework. "I wasn't sold when I saw it hanging. I thought sure, I'm an artist, but this is crazy over the top. Then I tried it on and—"

"It's you." Deidre gave a firm nod. "It's really you. I don't think most people could pull it off. Nor would they want to. Sean really knows his stuff, doesn't he?"

There were murmurs of agreement from all the women. Larissa rubbed her aching chest. She could remember that first rush of excitement. Joy. Anticipation. It didn't end in disappointment for everyone.

Just her.

Larissa pressed a hand to her quivering stomach. "When do we eat?"

13

Matt pulled open the door to the sprawling single-story house with a grin. "You made it. I wasn't sure you would."

Sean hadn't been sure, either. There were a million reasons not to have come and, despite a ton of thought, very few in favor. And yet, here he stood. "I can't stay late. I need to get back to Richmond tonight so I'm around for appointments tomorrow."

"Still glad you came. Is your friend coming?"

"Yeah, Toph is on his way." He'd run into Topher in Charlottesville, and they'd made plans to meet up for dinner after they each finished their errands. When Matt called with the invitation for nachos, Sean had used Topher as an excuse. Of course, Topher glommed onto the idea. Sean stepped into the foyer and glanced around. "This is a nice place."

"Right? I need to get Azure over here. Except I hate to get her hopes up if Jeremiah isn't interested in selling." Matt ran a hand through his hair. "Catch-22."

"Not really. Talk to Jeremiah and lay it out. He's not going to say anything to Azure if you're angling to surprise her."

"Isn't he required to tell Deidre? Like a marriage code or something?"

"What about my wife?" Jeremiah turned from the oven with a sloppy newlywed grin.

Matt sighed and leaned against the sparkling concrete countertop.

Sean waited a beat. When Matt didn't speak, he shook his head. Why did people make things complicated when they weren't? "Since you and Deidre are settled up at Peacock Hill, Matt's wondering if you're planning to sell this house."

"Sell? I hadn't—" Jeremiah cocked his head to the side. "You want to buy it?"

"I don't know. I mean, yes, I do, but Azure's never been here, so I don't know what she'd think. All I know is we can't live over my aunt and uncle's garage. That's a recipe for insanity." Matt shrugged. "It's not a big deal. There are other houses."

"Yeah. But you don't want to do renovations. And you don't want to be far from the garage." Jeremiah pushed some of the bowls and platters on the island away, making a larger space in front of him before turning to remove a sheet tray of cheese-covered chips from the oven. "Let me talk to Dee—I'll swear her to secrecy, if that helps—and I'll let you know this week?"

"Sure. There's no rush. We have a lot of time before we're married."

Sean choked on the root beer he was drinking. "Four months. You have four months before your wedding. That's not much time."

"Says the wedding planner." The doorbell rang and Matt snapped his mouth shut. "I'll get that before I say something that gets me in trouble with Azure."

Jeremiah snickered. "Four months isn't super short, is it?"

He could do it in that time-frame, but he liked to have more. Sean waggled his hand back and forth. "Depends. For them, it's enough, but it's not roomy. And buying a house can be stressful, especially when it's on top of planning a wedding."

"I'll make it as easy for them as I can." Jeremiah offered Sean a plate as Matt, Topher, Danny, and Duncan all clomped into the kitchen.

"Even Danny made it." Matt jabbed his friend's shoulder. "You've been scarce lately."

Danny reached around the group for a plate and wedged himself close to the counter so he could dish up chips. "Been busy."

"Dive on in, man." Jeremiah shook his head and passed plates to the others. "Don't be shy."

Red flooded Danny's face and he huffed out a breath. "Sorry. It's—I'm used to getting in and out as fast as I can these days. At least Claire isn't here to give me indigestion."

"Claire? What's wrong with Claire?" Matt reached for the spatula to load his plate with chips.

"That's what I'd like to know. We used to be friends, and now she treats me like I ran over her favorite cat." Danny scooped sour cream on top of his plate and edged toward the den. "Now that everyone's paired off, it's even more uncomfortable because we get thrown together. She's got a sharp tongue, and she knows how to use it."

Claire? Sean frowned as he fixed his plate. That wasn't like her. Of the ladies at Peacock Hill, he did most of his business with Claire, and she was cool and competent. It was practically impossible to ruffle her, no matter what he threw her way. "What'd you do to her?"

"Me? Nothing." Danny shoved a loaded chip in his mouth and chewed. After swallowing, he pointed at Sean. "Wedding planner guy, right?"

"That's me. Generally I go by Sean in less formal situations."

Topher laughed. "And I'm Topher—save you the trouble of

calling me the cake man or bakery boy or whatever catchy title you were thinking of."

"Sorry." Danny scooped another chip through the toppings on his plate. "Did you hear that other girl—the new one—is moving to Brazil at the end of the month?"

Sean's stomach knotted and he frowned down at his nachos. After Sunday, he'd hoped . . . well, so much for that.

"Who's the new girl? I'm out of the loop. I only recognize that guy," Topher pointed at Duncan, "and Sean."

"Larissa Carey." Sean cleared his throat and set his food aside. "I think you met with us for a cake tasting, but she went a different direction."

Topher nodded. "Then I probably don't remember her at all. What's in Brazil?"

"And how did you find that out?" Sean pinned Danny with his gaze.

"I thought we were meeting up at Peacock Hill The girls were talking about it before they redirected me here. I guess it's a big surprise to everyone." Danny shrugged. "It's too bad. She seemed nice."

Sean didn't like the gleam in Danny's eye. At all. Maybe it was good Larissa was heading to Brazil. She'd mentioned the possibility, but what had changed to make it official? Or was it? Maybe they'd just been talking about options. He wanted to know. He also wanted to give her space. He'd been determined not to make contact with her until she reached out to him. Had he made the wrong choice?

"Those are some loud thoughts. Care to share?" Topher's mutter was nearly lost under the conversation between Matt, Danny, and Jeremiah.

Did he? "I'm surprised, is all. Last I heard there wasn't anything official. Sounds like that's changed."

"And it's bad?"

"Not for her. This is what she wants—has wanted for a long time. Almost marrying Tom derailed it, and now she's getting back on track and chasing her dream. It's a good thing."

"Sorry, man. That stinks."

Sean stared at Topher. "No. No, it's okay. She—"

"Has no idea how you feel about her. I get it." Topher chuckled. "Maybe you should tell her before she goes. Give her something to think about on the plane."

If the kiss on Sunday hadn't done that for him, nothing was going to. The radio silence since then made it pretty clear she didn't feel the same way. "I already did that. There's nothing for her to think about."

"You should call Vanessa."

"What? No. I have zero interest in Vanessa."

"Right now. But who knows? Maybe someone great is hiding under her irritating, bossy, obnoxious shell, just waiting for the right person to help her out."

"Great sales pitch, but I'll pass. Besides, you see more of her than I do. If anyone's going to get together with Vanessa, it'll be you."

Topher shuddered. "I thought we were friends."

Sean grinned and pushed Larissa's impending trip to the back of his mind. "We are. So how about this—let's see if we can find a way to introduce Vanessa to Danny."

Topher snickered. "That's a plan."

SEAN KICKED off his loafers and glanced down at the slacks he'd worn to church. He could change, but it seemed like a lot of effort. Everything did. He'd managed to make it through nearly the entire month of May without going to check on Larissa at

Peacock Hill. Thinking about her was a different story. One thing at a time.

It didn't matter. From the bits and pieces he'd managed to wheedle out of Claire when he'd called to firm up retreat details, Larissa was flying to Brazil today. So that was that. It was good. Better than good. She wasn't available. Or maybe she wasn't interested. Either way, it worked out to the same thing. With her out of the country, maybe he could get back to his contented bachelor life. He'd never been one who felt he had to get married and have a family. Sure, it'd be nice, but marriage wasn't the only key to being happy. Maybe God was calling him to be single. If so, that was okay. As long as he could get over Larissa.

This was stupid.

Sean pushed himself off the couch and down the hall to his room. He wasn't going to sit here, moping the afternoon away. He'd go for a run. If that didn't get him out of this mood, he'd call Topher up and see if he wanted to play some basketball. Something—anything—to get him out of the house and away from the temptation to text Larissa one last time and wish her bon voyage.

He tossed his church clothes at the hamper and tugged on running shorts. He was reaching for a t-shirt when the doorbell chimed. Sean grabbed his socks and shoes and tugged the shirt over his head as he jogged to the door. With one arm in a sleeve, he yanked open the door and blinked. "Larissa."

"Oh. Um." Her gaze darted around. "Hi."

Sean finished pulling on his t-shirt and stepped back. Conflicting emotions tangled in his gut and he fought to keep his tone neutral. "Hi. You want to come in?"

She twisted her fingers together, hesitating on the doorstep. "Yeah. Sure. Were you leaving? I don't want to hold you up."

"Just going for a run. It'll keep. Come in. Do you want something to drink?" Did he have anything to drink? Water. There was obviously water, but did he even have powdered lemonade mix?

"No, I'm good. I won't keep you—I have a taxi waiting. I just wanted to stop and say goodbye. I don't even know if you know I'm leaving? And that seemed wrong, somehow." Larissa hovered in the little square of tile flooring that served as the apartment entryway.

Sean moved into the living room and waved at the couch. There had to be some way to get her to stay for a minute, didn't there? "Can you sit down for a minute?"

"Sure. He said he'd wait. It's not like I'm not paying."

"Right. Of course." Sean perched on the edge of a chair so he didn't crowd her on the couch. He cleared his throat. "Yes, I had heard you were leaving. Brazil, right? You're probably excited."

Her grin flashed as she settled onto the couch. "So excited. And the timing is good, too, since it's moving into winter there and will be in the mid-seventies."

Sean laughed. "Winter, huh? Nice."

"Right? Summer doesn't sound terrible though, to be honest. It seems like it's pretty temperate."

"I guess you'll find out."

"Probably not." Larissa frowned. "I have a three-month visa —it's strange and complicated. I don't really understand all the ins and outs, but the agency says this is the best they can do right now."

A tiny flicker of hope lit in his chest. Sean did his best to keep it from turning into more and aimed to keep his voice casual. "What will you do after Brazil?"

Larissa's gaze flicked up to his and held it. "I guess that sort of depends."

Could she hear his pounding heart too? Of course, she could mean anything with those words. Maybe she'd find another country to move to. Maybe Brazil would extend her visa. That could happen, right? "On what?"

"Having a reason to come back to the States." Larissa's tongue darted between her lips. "We haven't really talked since that kiss."

Mouth dry, all Sean could do was nod.

"I guess I thought you'd want to. But you never called. Or texted. Maybe I misunderstood."

"I figured the ball was in your court." He'd lost track of how many times he'd talked himself out of calling or texting.

"I guess I can see that." She fished her phone out of her pocket and glanced at the screen. "I should go. The thing is, I don't know what to do with that ball. I'm kind of scared to touch it, if I'm honest. I don't exactly have the best track record. I realize my timing is ridiculous, but maybe we could keep in touch and see what happens?"

What was going to happen when she was in a completely different hemisphere? "I'd like to keep in touch."

She cocked her head to the side. "But not see what happens?"

"I know what I want to happen. I guess I don't know how to bring that about when you're not around." Sean shrugged. How did you have a long distance relationship at the very start? On the flip side? If it was a possibility, he was willing to give it a shot.

A delicate pink washed over her cheeks as she stood and closed the distance between them. She hesitated before cradling his face in her hands and holding his gaze. "It's only fair to warn you, I'm going to need a lot of patience from you. I—the whole Tom thing—I don't know how to get over that and feel lovable again. I can't promise I ever will. So it may all come to nothing, but over the last month I realized that, like living and working overseas, I was always going to wonder if I didn't at least try."

"I can be patient." Sean lowered his forehead to hers and breathed in her subtle floral scent. "I'm in love with you."

Larissa jerked backward, head shaking. "Don't. You can't—that's a big word."

"I know. I've never said it to anyone outside my family before. That doesn't make it less true. I'm not telling you to pressure you or make you uncomfortable, but I thought you should know. This thing that we're trying out? I know where I want it to end—with you, walking down an aisle on your father's arm. And me, waiting for you at the front of the church."

Sean's heartbeats marked the time as she stared at him, dazed. Finally, she leaned forward and touched her lips to his in the barest whisper of a kiss.

"I have to go."

He nodded and reached for her hand. "Let me know when you get settled, okay?"

"I will."

He walked with her to the taxi and carefully shut the door when she was settled. Stepping back, he lifted a hand and watched her drive off. He'd laid his cards on the table. Hadn't meant to, but it had seemed right. Now he just had to figure out how to woo the woman he'd nearly scared away.

14

Dear Sean,

That seems like an awfully formal way to start an email, but everything else—and believe me, I tried six different things—was weird and stilted. Apparently, I'm even more awkward in email than in person. Who knew?

I'm sorry it's taken nearly a week for me to have a chance to write a longer note. I do want points for having let you know I was here. Especially since I emailed you and forgot to call my mom until the next day. To say she was displeased might be the world's biggest understatement. It did get her to switch from her old flip phone to a smart phone though, because that allows us to call over the Internet instead of dealing with international dialing.

Would you want to video chat sometime? I miss hearing your voice—which may be stupid. Is it stupid? It's not as if we talked all the time when we were in the same state. Still, the offer stands. Mom enjoyed being able to look out my window and see where I live. Maybe you would, too.

The little school where I'm teaching believes in throwing people in the moment they arrive. I don't mind, but it's not what I expected. (What did I expect? I'm not sure. Not this.) I have two classes—

mostly adults. No one speaks much English yet and the tiny bit of Spanish I know doesn't help as much as I'd hoped in the face of Portuguese. Everyone told me they were similar and I'd be fine. Either I'm dense, or everyone had a much different experience than I have so far.

Still, I'm meant to be teaching English and I don't have to know the language my students are speaking to do that. But it would help for the time I spend not teaching. That isn't as much time as you might think with only two classes. I still have most of my online students—and that was nearly full-time to begin with—and there are three private students who will take as much time as I can offer. These students, at least, are mostly practicing conversation, so time spent tutoring them is not really work.

And that brings us to my first Saturday in Brazil. I taught all three private students this morning before lunch, but now the rest of today and tomorrow stretch out like an empty canvas for me to fill. And I have no idea what to do.

In Richmond, before Tom, I was positive that teaching overseas would give me the opportunity to see all the sights around the world. I wanted to be that girl—the well-traveled one who, when someone mentions some far-off place, I could smile and say, "Oh, I was there. Didn't you love—" Now I have the chance and I'm terrified.

Everyone at my agency assured me Brazil—Sao Paulo in particular—was safe. Everyone at the school has warned me to be careful. I'm sure I'll be fine if I stick to well-populated tourist locations or sign up with some of the tour companies, but I can't quite take the step. Maybe it's a first-week thing and I'll laugh at myself this time next week. I guess I can hope.

So for today, I think I'm going to read on the tiny scrap of concrete that hangs off the side of the itsy-bitsy square that comprises my "apartment with balcony." Tomorrow? Who knows?

Larissa paused and drummed her fingers on the keyboard of her laptop. She scrolled up and reread the email. Was it too much like a diary rather than a friendly email? Could she even write a friendly email to a man who said he loved her? She glanced out the window at the sprawling city. From in here, she could basically be in any major city. Was this what she wanted?

Peacock Hill had seemed twelve thousand miles from civilization, but now she was in the middle of the city surrounded by people chattering in other languages, her heart craved the quiet. Tears pricked her eyes. Was she ever going to be content?

Larissa forced her attention back to the email. How was she supposed to end it? The breezy "Respectfully" she put at the end of her work emails was too impersonal. On the flip side, was "Yours" too much? She wasn't going to use "love" as if it didn't matter. Not after his declaration. He might insist he wasn't waiting for her to say it back to him, but that had to be a lie. Nobody threw out the big "L" without hoping for a response in kind. She sighed.

Let me know about scheduling time for a video call. I'm three hours ahead of you, so if we can try for after three your time, it'd be helpful. –Larissa

Good enough. He'd notice the lack of a proper closing. Sean was the kind of guy who noticed things like that. Would he comment on it? Did it matter? She clicked send and pushed away from the small table that served as a desk and dining area.

The tiny apartment came with her job. It was one room—if she discounted the shower and toilet, which were enclosed in a space smaller than her linen closet had been back home. The main room held a sink beside a two-foot-wide stretch of counter. Her hotplate sat on top of that counter, the mini-fridge beneath. Throw in the table, two chairs, a three-drawer dresser, and a bed, and the space was full. She'd never been an adventurous cook, but she hadn't been one to eat out all the time. That was going to change here in Brazil.

It was a good way to try new foods. Right?

"I said I was going to read on the balcony. So that's what I'm going to do." Talking to herself. Aloud. Fabulous.

Larissa tugged open the sliding door, wincing as the metal screeched. She dragged the straight-backed chair close enough that she could prop her feet on the metal rail and nodded. It wasn't elegant, but it would do.

~

"You're all fancy." Larissa studied the tie knotted at Sean's collar, just visible at the bottom of the phone screen. Maybe a video call wasn't as good as talking in person, but it still beat email. "That's the tie you wore to our first meeting."

Sean's eyebrows lifted. "You remember what tie I wore?"

Her cheeks heated. She'd thought entirely too much about Sean in the first stages of planning her wedding to Tom. Tom, of course, hadn't noticed. At the time, she'd believed it was because he was secure in their relationship, so it didn't matter if she thought someone was attractive. Now? It was obvious he probably hadn't cared. Better to play it off. "Apparently."

"Interesting. As it turns out, this is the tie I usually wear to consultations. Not on purpose. Just happens that way. Or it's a subconscious thing."

"It's Sunday. You don't work on Sunday."

"As a rule, you're right, I don't. But these clients have been trying to find a time to meet and talk for almost a full month. They're busy during the week and I'm slammed on the weekends, so it seemed prudent to make an exception if there was going to be any chance of us working together."

"And is there?"

Sean tugged at his tie, working it loose. He flicked open the top button of his shirt and his image on the screen bobbled. "I don't know. I guess it's up to them."

"Isn't it always?"

He flashed a grin. "Yeah. This case, even more so. It's two guys."

"Two . . . huh. You'd do that?"

"I told Topher I'd talk to them. They're friends of his. I gave them my usual spiel—we'll see what they decide."

His usual—oh. She chuckled. "Tom was startled by that conversation. He pushed—sort of—for us to find someone else. I guess he was hoping he'd talk me into moving in with him as we got closer to the wedding. He certainly tried."

Sean nodded. "I've been told I lose a lot of business because of it, but I can't in good conscience not lay out my views on the purpose of marriage."

"You could leave out the part about sex before marriage being sin. Hardly anyone thinks that way today. Even in the church. It's old fashioned." Larissa wasn't sure she believed it. She hadn't slept with Tom—or anyone—but that was more because it hadn't seemed right than from any sense that God would care. She'd always figured it would happen when the right guy came around.

The corners of Sean's mouth turned down. "Anyway, I explained that I wouldn't knowingly work with a couple who were openly living together. They asked for the names of a heterosexual couple I turned away. I gave them four. So maybe at least they won't take me to court for discrimination. It's not so much about them being gay as it is willingly helping someone sin."

"Assuming being gay is sin."

His frown became more pronounced. "Are you baiting me, or do you really believe that?"

"I don't know. I guess it's not our place to judge, you know? We're supposed to love people and let God sort them out."

"If you were about to walk in front of a truck, should I stop you? We're called to love others. The most loving thing we can do is help people find Jesus. He came to Earth to die for our sin —which means admitting we're sinners and repenting. How can we do that if no one explains what sin is and why we need to repent? If I don't, I'm allowing them to remain blind and condemned to hell."

"That's a little harsh, isn't it? You really think a loving God is going to send people to hell?"

"He's not the one sending them—it's their choice. God is holy. He can't countenance sin. But He loved us too much to leave us to die for them, and that's why He sent Jesus. He loves us enough to save us, if we let Him. But it's always our choice."

Larissa let her gaze drift away from her phone's screen to the skyline of Sao Paulo outside her window. This wasn't the conversation she'd expected. "What if they're born that way?"

"You struggle with swearing, right?"

A flippant response hovered on the tip of her tongue, but she swallowed it and nodded.

"You know it's not what God wants, right?"

The verse her mother had made her memorize flitted through her mind. *Do not let any unwholesome talk come out of your mouths . . .* "Yeah."

"Just because we accept Jesus as our Savior, we don't stop having to wrestle with sin. The apostle Paul talks about the thorn in his flesh. Everyone has sin they have to fight—it doesn't matter what the sin is. What's important is that we choose to fight it and ask Jesus to help us."

"I guess. I still—I mean, most people know, right? So what's the point in saying something? You just come across as judgmental. It's not loving. Or kind. Jesus didn't go around pointing out people's sin. He just loved them."

Sean snorted. "Seriously? When he told the woman caught in adultery to go and sin no more, what was He doing? Look, I get it. We're not supposed to walk around sticking our fingers in people's faces and yelling that they're sinners. And we need to be constantly aware of and confessing our own sins—and working to do better. At the same time, I do think we have to take a stand and tell people the truth, especially when staying silent would make us complicit."

Could you be complicit in someone else's sin? Wasn't it their choice?

"It's a little different for me. I have a business built around providing a service to Christian couples. I don't, generally, work with people who aren't believers, so I'm not trying to hold non-Christians to the Bible's standards."

"Aren't you, though? Is either of the guys you met with today a believer?"

He sighed. "No. I get what you're saying. Part of why I haven't been rushing to make my schedule clear to meet with these guys is exactly this. I'm torn. They aren't believers, so it's not surprising that their lifestyle is sinful. But at the same time, they're asking me to help them plan to continue in that sinful lifestyle. I want them to have all the information about why I'm not comfortable with the idea. I wouldn't help a man set up his mistress in an apartment he keeps from his wife. I wouldn't knowingly help someone sin."

"Why'd you even meet with them? It sounds like you should've just said no."

"Topher asked. I guess they've been running into trouble finding the help they need. Maybe it's a chance to show them Jesus. I don't know. I've been praying about it. A lot. And I keep coming back to the idea that I shouldn't help someone persist in their sin."

"That's tough. I hope you can figure it out." Larissa winced. She was probably supposed to say something more spiritual, but right now that wasn't happening. She was trying to pray. Trying to believe God cared one way or the other about her life. But it was a challenge.

"Thanks. I'll keep praying. That's all I can do right now." He blew out a breath. "Did you enjoy church in Brazil?"

Heat washed over her cheeks. "I didn't go. I'm not even sure how you find a church in a new country."

"The Internet?"

Yeah, fine, she could have done a search. Or asked at school —there were a couple of other teachers there she was pretty sure were believers from snippets of their classes she'd over-heard as she walked past. "I'll find somewhere for next week, okay? Promise."

"You don't have to do it for me. I just assumed." Sean's gaze veered away from the phone's screen then back. "What are we doing, Larissa?"

Everything in her went cold. "What do you mean?"

He scrubbed a hand over his face. "Where do you think this can go? Best case?"

"You said you loved me." It wasn't an answer to his question. She didn't know how to answer his question. Best case? Marriage, a house in the suburbs, and two-point-four kids. Maybe a cat. But it was a long way from this not-quite-dating thing to marriage and a family.

"I do. That doesn't have to factor in, though. If you don't— can't—feel the same way. Or if you've decided that believing in Jesus isn't for you."

Ah. She should have guessed. "So I have to go to church to believe? Who made you the Christianity police all of the sudden?"

"That's not what I said. Not what I'm trying to be. But you have to admit church hasn't been a priority for you since April."

Since Tom. He was too polite to say it that way. "I've been struggling. I haven't lied about that. I still believe in Jesus. But

I'm not sure that's a two-way street. It's a big world with a lot of people in it. Does He really have time for me? To worry about the little things in my life? I'm saved. Maybe that's the end of where He cares."

"I hope you know that's not true. Even if it feels true."

"Don't tell me to consider the lilies, okay? That seems to be what everyone wants to toss my way." A weight settled on her, as if something heavy sat on her chest. Sean acted like he had all the answers. All she had were questions. He said he loved her—and she wanted to give in and love him back—but could she do that with him so unwilling to budge on so much?

"I'm sorry you're hurting. I'll keep praying for you."

She nodded. A perfect answer. Obviously sincere. Sean was a good man. Her eyes were burning with unshed tears. "I—maybe I don't deserve to ask this, but please don't give up on me."

"I won't. God hasn't, either."

Larissa nodded. "Maybe we can call again later?"

"I'd like that."

She said goodbye and tapped the end button before letting her head drop back and closing her eyes. Hot tears rolled down her cheeks, and her breath clogged in her chest. She'd come to Brazil to get her life back on track after the disastrous detour of her relationship with Tom. Even as she'd planned for—and looked forward to—her marriage, she'd resented the fact that she wasn't going to travel. Now she was living abroad and all she could think about was a settled life in Virginia with Sean.

What was wrong with her?

15

"Hey man, you made it." Duncan tossed a can of soda at Sean. "You're early, even."

Sean caught the can and popped the top. "When I didn't get a couple wanting a July fourth wedding by mid-October, I blocked it out. I think people were less excited about the date because it's a Thursday."

"I don't get wanting a national holiday for your anniversary."

"Hey." Azure frowned at Duncan from across the as-yet-unlit bonfire. "Sometimes holiday weekends make sense."

"Says the Labor Day bride." Sean chuckled and settled on one of the logs that served as seating out in the bonfire area. "I'm surprised there's no event here today."

"Like you said, Thursday. Plus we're not exactly near any amazing fireworks. You have to go into Charlottesville or over to Waynesboro for that. Throw in the big two-week retreat that checks in on Saturday and I don't think anyone's upset." Duncan glanced over at his sister who was manning the grill. "Deidre's freaked about the retreat."

"Why? She's had a handful of them already this summer. What's different with this one?" Sean shifted. Logs were less comfortable than he remembered them from his camping days. Or maybe he'd gone soft. Maybe a combination. "Y'all need to put some real chairs out here."

Duncan snorted. "That's what I keep telling Dee. She says this is more rustic. I haven't gotten splinters in my rear yet, but I'm expecting them any moment."

"What are you two talking about?" Jeremiah eyed the logs before lowering himself to the ground and using the wood as a backrest.

"Why's Deidre worried about this upcoming retreat?" This wasn't one Sean had arranged. He'd flipped through his mental files and come up blank. He was still primarily dealing with weddings, though he had a few weekend reunions toward the end of the month. August was primarily youth group retreats and back-to-school events, with only two weddings. His work often tapered off for the fall and settled into planning versus execution, with an uptick again between Thanksgiving and Christmas.

"I think because it's the first event that's been one hundred percent hers. Well, hers and Claire's. The organization contacted her directly through the website and had no outside —or in-house—event planning." Jeremiah shrugged. "Her nerves got me kicked off the grill. She said it was soothing to flip burgers."

"Takes all kinds. I'm happy to let her cook if that's what she needs. Anna and I have been so slammed with landscaping jobs lately I'm happy to sit anytime I can."

Jeremiah nodded at Duncan. "I hear you. That storm last week kicked up the calls I was getting for repair work. Trying to balance that with the regular lawn customers has been hectic."

"You need us to pick up some slack? I have a couple of guys who could probably use a few extra hours." Duncan dug out his cell phone and tapped at the screen.

"I might take you up on that until I get clear from repairing storm damage. Can you shoot me names and numbers?"

Duncan swiped and tapped at his phone. "Done. I'll let them know to be on the lookout for contact from you. They need to bring their own mowers?"

"Yeah. That still work?"

Duncan nodded.

"Food's ready," Deidre hollered from the grill before stretching her arms up over her head. "Might as well eat. Everyone else will get here when they can. Where's Anna?"

Duncan stood and dusted off his shorts. "She got overheated today and was going to rest a bit before dinner. I'm not sure she'll come, to be honest."

"Oh." Disappointment oozed around Deidre's words.

"I can call and let her know she needs to come."

Deidre shook her head at Duncan's offer. "Don't do that. Maybe I'll stop by on the way back to the main house."

"Sure. You okay?"

Deidre and Jeremiah exchanged a glance before she nodded. "I wanted to tell everyone at the same time, but with Anna not here and Claire bailing, I guess that's not happening."

"Claire bailed? Why?" Duncan grabbed a paper plate and started loading it with food.

"I mentioned Danny was going to come and she suddenly had too much to do to get ready for Saturday. I don't really blame her. He's been seeing that girl in Charlottesville for almost six weeks."

"And he doesn't shut up about it, either." Jeremiah reached for a plate. "Even I'm getting annoyed."

Sean tried to follow the conversation, but his exposure to Danny was minimal. He liked Claire, though. She was another organized soul. Event planning suited her to the ground and the two of them thought a lot alike. Why couldn't he have fallen in love with someone like her? "So it's bad Danny's dating someone?"

Azure scoffed. "Danny's always dating someone. Usually a lot of someones. That was easier. Now that he's shown he can have a long-term, committed relationship, it's just worse for Claire."

"Because . . . ?" Sean got in line for the food. "I'm lost."

"Claire has a thing for Danny. Danny's clueless." Azure reached for a hot dog and dropped it on her plate. "I think she could do better, but she hasn't asked my opinion."

"Sorry I'm late." Matt jogged up the slight hill to the bonfire area and reached for Azure's hand. He pulled her close and kissed her. "Got a new rebuild dropped off at the garage right after you left. Gorgeous car—definitely going to be a fun project."

"Referral from the Porsche guy?" Azure reached for another plate and handed it to Matt.

He nodded.

Azure beamed at him and moved away from the food to sit on a log.

Sean finished loading his burger and scooped some potato salad from a bowl. "You restore cars?"

Matt nodded. "It's a side business. The garage isn't completely self-sustaining. Small town, you know? This is a reasonable way to get some extra income and keep the garage open. Plus it's fun."

"That's great man." Duncan carried his food back to his seat and eyed his sister. "You said tell everyone—what's the news?"

Pink tinged Deidre's cheeks and she exchanged another glance with Jeremiah. "It's not a big—"

"We're expecting." Jeremiah reached for Deidre's hand and pulled her close. "She's been trying to figure out how to tell people for over a week."

Duncan grinned and shot to his feet, knocking over his plate and spilling food onto the ground. He started to pick it up, shook his head, and grabbed his sister in a hug. "Congrats! That's great news."

Jeremiah laughed and nudged Duncan with his elbow. "Can I have my wife back?"

"You need a hug, too?"

"I'm good." Jeremiah bumped his fist to Duncan's. "But I appreciate the thought."

Azure and Matt chimed in with congratulations. Sean tossed in his as well. It seemed fast, but if they were excited, who was he to say anything? They'd gotten married in December. Six months. That . . . was not what he'd jump into.

"How's Larissa doing?" Deidre brought her plate over and sat beside Sean. She patted the log and Jeremiah joined her.

"Good. She has another two months in Brazil. We email a lot and try to do a video call on Sunday afternoons. With the time difference and work schedules, that's the easiest to coordinate." Sean studied his food. He wasn't any clearer about where things stood between the two of them. Was he supposed to mention that?

"What will she do when her time in Brazil is up? She'd mentioned the Ukraine one time when she was here."

Sean shrugged. "It's up in the air. She hasn't said it outright, but I get the feeling she doesn't love living abroad as much as she thought she would."

"Maybe it's Brazil, and she'd like somewhere else better?"

"Possible. But the things she says aren't country-specific. I think she liked the idea of it more than the reality. To be honest, I think she'd rather be teaching elementary school again rather than just teaching English." The problem, of course, was figuring out how to suggest that. She had a plan in place and, having set it aside for Tom, so now she was determined to see it through. "She's mentioned the possibility of heading back to the States. I guess we'll see what happens."

"How are you doing?"

Sean met Deidre's knowing gaze and sighed. "I'm okay. She feels like this is something she has to do. What am I supposed to say?"

"You could go visit her."

Right. Just pop off to Brazil for the weekend. Putting aside the fact that he didn't have a passport, this wasn't the time of year when his schedule allowed for spontaneous travel to a foreign country. He shook his head.

"Well, it's a thought." Deidre picked up her burger and took a bite.

"Sure." He glanced down at his plate and stabbed a couple of potato pieces with his fork. Time to change the subject. He was ready for an hour when he wasn't thinking about Larissa. The gang at Peacock Hill was usually pretty good at distracting him. "Tell me about the group that's coming and why you're freaked out."

"Good to see you again, Sean."

Sean glanced up from his laptop and reached for the files he had spread on the cafe table around him. "Hey, Azure. Matt. Thanks for coming out. This place has an agreement with a couple of different caterers, so it's a nice place to do tastings without having to go to a ton of separate places. Let me clear all this out of the way, and I'll let them know we're ready."

Azure and Matt sat while Sean slid his files into his messenger bag. After tucking the bag under the table, he stood and crossed to the counter. It took a moment to catch the manager's eye, but she finally saw him and nodded.

Sean returned to the table. "You're determined to do burgers and hot dogs on the grill for the food, right?"

"Labor Day, man. I don't think you can have anything else." Matt spread his hands on the table. "Plus it's fun. And it's a nod to our first date. Sort of."

"What he's trying to say is yes, we're certain. And making the burgers ahead of the time is easy enough. Deidre, Claire, and Anna said they'd pitch in."

"And Aunt Ida."

"Right. And Matt's aunt. Which means the food is well and truly covered. With Aunt Ida on our team, we'd be set for a wedding six times the size."

Sean laughed. Mrs. Patterson was certainly a force to be reckoned with. If she was taking on the wedding catering, he wasn't going to spend any more time worrying about it. "Let me know if you need me to handle anything on that end. Otherwise, I'm going to trust that you've got it under control. So we're just tasting cake today. I have three bakers coming. If you don't like any of them, I have some others I can arrange for another day. Or you can visit their bakeries on your own if you'd rather. These are my top three, so I suspect you're going to be happy with one of them."

"No pressure, right?" Matt grinned.

"Absolutely none." Sean gestured for Topher to come ahead. "Matt, Azure, this is Topher Adams. You might remember him from Duncan and Anna's wedding. Topher, Matt Patterson and Azure Hewitt."

"Hi. Pleasure to meet you." Topher set down a tray filled with cake samples and extended his hand. "I'm sure Matt told you I have another Labor Day event already, so I probably won't be available to set up and serve on site, but I have some contractors I use who do an amazing job. There's no problem with making the cake—just the onsite."

Sean frowned. He'd planned to wait and only tell them if it mattered. Topher always wanted all the information to be out on the table right at the very beginning of everything. Sean appreciated honesty, but sometimes it was okay to wait until people needed information. All things considered, Topher was Sean's pick for what Matt and Azure were looking for in a cake. Hopefully Topher hadn't just blown it.

"What we have here are my four most popular cake flavors, eight different fillings, and five icing options. You can mix and match however you want .If you like a filling and want that flavor carried over into the icing, I can usually do that. Let's start with the white cake." Topher put a small plastic cup holding a generous bite-sized square of cake in front of both Matt and Azure.

Sean listened to the spiel with one ear and ran through his mental calendar. Squeezing Matt and Azure in today had been difficult. His Saturday bride was turning into a diva and he fully expected her to demand his undivided attention from Wednesday. She had the means to pay his rates, which was usually nice, but his other July brides weren't as squared away as he liked to have them, and it would've been better to give them some extra time this week.

He dragged his attention back to the task at hand and noted preferences as Matt and Azure commented. Couples typically ended up confused after the second baker. It was part of his job to make sure they remembered what they did and didn't care for with each vendor. Often, it was only Sean's notes that helped them remember what combinations were available from which bakers when they sat down to make a final decision after all the tastings were done.

Matt and Azure spent nearly three hours—an hour per baker, and twice as long as he'd budgeted—but left having made a decision. It was good to have one more check on the list of things that needed to be completed for their wedding. It was only seven weeks until Labor Day. Most of the prep was done, but he hated leaving cake this late. They were fortunate he'd been able to convince the three bakers to take on another client this close to the date.

"How'd it go?" Topher slid into the empty seat across from Sean and set a tall mug of coffee in front of him. He sipped from his own mug.

"They made a choice. I'll be calling with their order later."

"Me?"

Sean nodded. "Like you're surprised. You know you're the best out there, right?"

Topher's cheeks colored and he shrugged. "I'm always grateful for business. It seems it could all disappear in a flash, and I'd never have seen it coming. I don't take it for granted. Not with the DIY shows on TV convincing people to bake their own and the trend toward non-traditional reception desserts like donut cakes."

"I guess that makes sense. I'm always a little amazed so many people want a wedding planner. It's not that hard to plan your own wedding, if you're organized. But it's still nice when people decide they'd rather I did it."

"Yeah. I talked with Brian and Dave."

Ah. There was a reason for this conversation that went beyond friendly chat. Sean had seen Topher leave after he finished his part of the afternoon. He'd probably had someone behind the counter give him a call when they saw Matt and Azure exit. This was the kind of place where people would do that for you. Friendly. Obliging. Somewhat meddlesome. "Yeah?"

"They seemed—let's go with surprised—by your initial interview."

"I imagine they were. It's what I talk about with everyone, though."

Topher nodded. "I get that. So do they, actually. They're still tempted to go with you. They asked my opinion. I wasn't sure what to say. I mean, if I were going to get married, I'd want you to plan my wedding. At the same time, I don't know that I'd want to work with someone who was so clearly uncomfortable with my choices."

"Exactly. There are a lot of other wedding planners. Probably some who'd fall over themselves to work with a gay couple to prove how open-minded and progressive they were."

"You're not wrong. They've been approached by one who offered to do it for free."

"Why wouldn't they jump on that? Wedding planners aren't cheap."

Topher laughed. "It's true. Brian said he didn't like the vibe. I guess it felt like the guy was trying to use them as a statement piece."

"I wouldn't like that, either. I'll be honest. I've been praying they'll choose someone else. I know I left it open—their decision. But man, I don't know if I can do it."

"Dave wondered about that. He's pushing for them to just do it themselves. Can I ask why?"

"Why what?"

"Why you don't think you could work with them."

Sean sighed. Would he be able to explain it to Topher any better than he had to Larissa? "I guess it boils down to not being able to escape the sense that I'd be contributing to their sin. It'd be like helping someone plan to cheat or steal. I can't do that."

"Okay. I can see that. You've gotta listen to the Holy Spirit. I'll nudge them in another direction."

"You don't have to do that. If they come to me, I can turn them down."

Topher shook his head. "Nah. Then it becomes an issue, and you have to try and explain it to them. Right now they're impressed with you. They don't agree with your standpoint, but they appreciate that you're willing to state it aloud. I guess you did it in such a way that it wasn't offensive."

"I tried. I wanted to make sure they understood that it wasn't them—as people—that I had an issue with. They're created in the image of God the same way I am. They have a sin nature the same as I do. They need Jesus. The same as I do."

"And that is why, despite everything, they were considering going with you. Why can't more people have that mindset? The understanding that sin—whatever form it takes—doesn't take away from the fact that we're still God's creation."

"To be fair, sometimes Christians get so caught up in sin being wrong that *we* lose track of the fact that we're all sinners made in God's image. In the face of that? I'm not surprised non-believers look at us and see self-righteous hypocrites. On the flip side, it feels like non-believers assume the worst of anyone who loves Jesus. Then we swing too far the other direction and become scared to call sin sin. It's tricky. I don't know if it can be solved. I'm just trying to figure out a way to love people without compromising my witness." Sean took a long sip from his coffee.

"That's all we can do." Topher drummed his fingers on the table. "One more question."

"Sure."

"I heard you might be heading off to Brazil sometime soon."

"What? Where'd you hear that?"

Topher shrugged. "Little bird told me. What's in Brazil?"

A little bird. The only people who knew about Larissa—in any way—were the gang at Peacock Hill. But Topher didn't know any of them. He'd worked one wedding there. One. With Vanessa. "You've been talking to Vanessa."

"Not by choice, believe me. But in one of her hours of endless monologuing, she happened to mention it."

"Well, she has her information wrong. I'm not going to Brazil." Sean drained his coffee and set the mug down. "I'm not sure there'd be any point."

"Because?"

"Because Larissa . . .I don't know if anything can happen there. No matter how much I want it to."

"At the risk of sounding repetitive, because?"

"Because I'm not sure she wants what I want. I want the whole deal. Marriage. A family. Roots. She wants to travel and see the world. Move from place to place every time her contract runs out." Maybe that wasn't completely accurate. When they'd spoken two days ago, she'd sounded tired and homesick. And lonely. "She says she misses me, then turns around and talks about how great Brazil is. I don't exactly have a portable career. It takes time to get established somewhere. To make contacts. I can't uproot myself every time she gets a wild hair."

"When's she's talking about Brazil, is she gushing? Telling you all the stuff you really ought to see? Or just saying how great it is—like she's trying to convince herself?"

That was a ridiculous idea. Wasn't it? He thought through their conversation and a flicker of hope kindled in his heart. "You think it's possible?"

"Anything's possible. I guess the question is whether or not you think it is." Topher studied Sean a moment. "Sure you're not going to Brazil?"

"Positive. No passport."

"Seriously?"

"I've never needed it. I don't see the point in having it when I have no plans to travel outside the country."

Topher pointed his finger. "You need to fix that. You marry a woman like Larissa? You're going to be leaving the country. Even if you two have to struggle to make it work for your schedules—teacher vacations are notoriously good times for weddings."

"I'll think about it."

"Do that." Topher slid his chair back and stood. "I'll talk to Dave and Brian. Keep me posted about Larissa, would you? I never watched soap operas, but I begin to see their appeal."

Sean snorted. Great. His life had devolved into a plot for daytime TV. It did have the high points. Jilted bride, unrequited love, running away to a foreign country. All that it needed was a love triangle. Not that he watched the shows. Much. Anymore.

He scrubbed a hand over his face. Maybe that's what got him into this mess in the first place. Now he'd just keep praying God would make it clear what was supposed to happen next.

16

Larissa collapsed onto her bed and let out the groaning sigh that had been building in her chest all day. She hated living here. Keeping up the cheerful and effervescent persona of someone living the dream took all her energy. She'd made a few day trips—even hooked up with a group of expat Americans. But not even immersion into a group who adored Brazil and everything it had to offer could mask the truth any longer.

This lifestyle was not for her.

It wasn't even that changing locations would fix things. It wasn't Brazil's fault. If she'd been here on vacation with someone she loved, she'd probably love it. And that, right there, was the problem.

Yes, she'd made a few friends, but none of them were the kind of friend that kept in touch. She had to make all the effort. That was exhausting, too. At home, she'd had friends who sought her out. Okay, they'd fallen by the wayside once she and Tom had gotten engaged. Tom's fault—although she'd allowed it. But when they'd heard about the jilting, they'd reached out, although Larissa had been too ashamed to reciprocate. Even the gang at Peacock Hill had been friendlier to her than her so-called friends, and it didn't look as if anyone in Brazil was going to become a fast friend either.

She wanted to go home. To reconnect.

To see Sean.

He'd sent her several hilarious emails with exploits in cake tastings this week. Four different couples who'd all chosen the exact same flavor combinations. Sean said he didn't know the actual probability of that, but he hadn't thought it was high. She'd laughed more from his description of the events and how he'd seen it start to happen, had even, in two cases, tried to steer them in different directions based on their initial reactions, all to no avail. It was normal and silly. The kind of conversation couples had when they were sitting on the sofa at the end of a long day.

She'd never had anything close to that with Tom. He'd pushed aside her questions about his job, saying he liked to leave the office at the office. At the time, it had seemed considerate. After all, didn't marriage coaches say people should leave the stress of their days behind and focus on the family when they got home? Over time, Larissa had realized work was a part of his life Tom kept her out of.

There had to be a balance. And telling Sean her frustrations with students or the administration helped her move through them so she could be better at her job. She'd never felt she could share about her work with Tom—not when he'd been so adamant about leaving his work at the office. Now she realized how much she'd shaped herself into the person Tom wanted her to be. And how far that was from the person God made her.

Someone knocked on the door.

She could ignore it. Just lie here and pretend she wasn't

home. It might be Friday night, but she wasn't in the mood to go dancing or sit in a small smoky cafe drinking coffee. Those were two activities her friends here enjoyed. A couple of people liked to go to the movies, but they were into Portuguese art films. Reading subtitles was never going to be her thing.

Another knock, louder this time.

With a sigh, she pushed herself up and crossed to the door. She looked through the peephole and froze. Tom? She squeezed her eyes closed and opened them again, but the picture didn't change. Tom was standing outside her door, lifting his hand to knock a third time. He wasn't going to go away, no matter how well she played possum.

Larissa yanked open the door and frowned. "What?"

"Hi, baby."

"Baby? Don't baby me. What are you doing here, Tom? You're in Brazil. You realize that, right?" She'd tried to convince him to consider South America for their honeymoon, but he'd been determined to go on a cruise. He'd said the honeymoon was his to decide, and a cruise was more romantic. "Last I checked, Brazil is part of South America. An entire continent you condemned as, oh, what was it you said?"

Red crawled up his throat. "I was wrong, okay? Can I come in?"

"No."

He blinked and started to step forward.

"I said no." Larissa closed the door some, wedging herself in the small opening. "What do you want?"

Tom held up his hands and stepped back. "I just want to talk. I made a mistake, babe. These last three months have been torture."

A mistake? She snorted. "A mistake is wearing navy blue socks with black pants, not leaving the woman who wanted to spend her life with you at the altar without even having the courtesy to tell her yourself."

"Shh. You don't have to yell. I get it. You're upset. But we can move past that. I'm sorry. I'll say I'm sorry as many times as I need to for you to forgive me. Just keep your voice down. Let me in, okay? We can talk about this."

"Stop telling me what to do! Maybe I don't want to keep my voice down. Maybe I don't care if all my neighbors know the creep I'd planned to marry is here trying to get me to take him back." Larissa stepped back and started to close the door. "Bye, Tom. Enjoy Brazil."

He stuck his foot in the doorway. "Come on, Larissa. Can't we at least talk?"

"What's there to say? You left me at the altar. I'm not sure how we move past that. Do you have any idea how humiliating —not to mention expensive—it was to mail back all the wedding gifts? Go away." Her eyes burned. How was she not done crying over him?

Tom pushed on the door and she fought to hold strong. He was going to get in—there was no way for her to hold him off if he decided to put his weight behind it. *Jesus! Help me, please.* The prayer was instinct and even as she thought it, Larissa frowned. Why would He answer now?

"Come on, babe. I said I was sorry." Tom leaned against the door. His breath was hot on her face.

She put her whole body weight against the door and kicked at his toes. "I'm not interested. I forgive you. I do. These past months I've realized we weren't ready to get married. In some ways, you did both of us a favor. Did you ever love me?"

"What? Of course I did. Do. I still love you."

Larissa shook her head and leaned harder against the door as Tom's force increased against it. "No, you don't. I don't know why you're here, but that's not it. I saw the pictures of you on our honeymoon. You weren't lacking for company."

He managed to look sheepish. "I made a mistake. I've already said I'm sorry. Let me come in. We'll talk."

"No." She slipped backward as he pushed against the door. He was going to get in and there was nothing she could do about it. He'd never been violent when they were dating. Maybe he'd leave it at talking. Except, if he was willing to just talk, wouldn't he go away when she asked him to? "Please. Go away."

"Larissa! Hi!" A voice echoed down the hall.

Startled, Tom stepped back and stuffed his hands in his pockets.

Larissa wanted to slam the door shut and bolt it, but instead leaned her head out to see who had called out. It was Kevin and Renee, one of the handful of Christians she'd run into in Brazil. They were a little older and happily married, so she hadn't sought out a lot of time with them. Why were they here? "Hi, Renee. Kevin."

"We were in the neighborhood and thought we'd see if you wanted to grab dinner." Renee glanced at Tom. "Unless you have plans?"

"No. No plans. Tom was just leaving." She glared at Tom. "Right?"

"Apparently. This isn't over. I came to Brazil for you." Tom nodded at Kevin and Renee before stalking down the hall.

"Are you okay?" Renee reached out and put her hand on the door. "Larissa?"

The trembling started in her knees and she sank to the floor. A sob tore from her throat.

"Hey. Shh." Renee squatted down and rubbed Larissa's arm. "Can you scoot back so we can come in?"

Larissa gave a jerky nod and scooched back enough that

Kevin and Renee could enter. Kevin shut the door behind them and twisted the lock.

"Can I get you something? Water?" Kevin glanced around and stepped to the kitchen area. He opened the small fridge and got a bottle of water. "Or I can make tea? If you have it?"

"This is fine." Larissa fought to keep her voice steady. The tremors had subsided, somewhat. "I'm so embarrassed."

"Why? You weren't doing anything wrong. Can I ask who that was?" Renee shifted on the floor so she was cross-legged.

"My ex-fiancé, Tom."

"What did he want?" Kevin lowered himself to the floor and rested his hand on Renee's leg. It was one of the things Larissa had noticed about them—they were always in contact with one another. Maybe it was something small, like this, but Kevin seemed to go out of his way to remind his wife that he was there and he loved her. It was yet another example of how ill-suited she and Tom had been. She'd tried to hold his hand when they'd been walking to the car after dinner only once. He'd pushed her away, making it clear that public affection—even something as simple as holding hands—wasn't okay. Why hadn't she known better than to keep seeing him?

Larissa uncapped the water and took a long drink. "To talk. Or so he said. But we don't have anything to talk about, and he wouldn't leave when I asked. Why are you here?"

Renee and Kevin exchanged a glance before Kevin spoke. "We were in the neighborhood. You mentioned where you lived, you remember?"

Larissa nodded.

"There's a new restaurant a few blocks down. We've wanted to try it since it opened."

Renee had mentioned it. It had never gone as far as making plans to meet up, but the suggestion was out that they should. Larissa had taken it as one of those polite but non-committal invitations no one intended to follow up on. "But why are you here?"

"As we were walking past your building, I felt a strong nudge that we should come up and see if you wanted to join us." Renee looked down. "But I didn't say anything to Kevin."

"We were maybe a half-block up and I stopped and asked her if she was feeling the same thing I was." Kevin shrugged. "When she admitted she was, we turned around and headed back. The sense of urgency grew as we got closer and when we saw that guy leaning on your door, Renee called out."

"I'm grateful." Tears burned Larissa's eyes. "But I don't understand."

"I think it was the Holy Spirit telling us to come."

Had He really heard her prayer and cared enough to answer? A tear slipped down her cheek. Then another. *Thank you, Jesus.* "I did. I wasn't sure He cared anymore, though. Do you ever feel like God's silent?"

"There have been times, sure. Usually I discover I only feel like He's silent when I've stopped listening."

Larissa looked at Renee. Was that the problem? She didn't have to ask—the resonance in her soul said it all. It was so easy to get caught up in doing. She was smart and capable and had been raised to have a plan and put it into action. It didn't leave a lot of room for waiting for God to speak.

"Sound about right?" Kevin cocked his head to the side.

"Yeah, it does." Larissa heaved out a breath. "Did I say thank you?"

Renee chuckled. "You did. And you're welcome. Now, since I dislike lying, even in a good cause, what about that dinner?"

"No. I appreciate the offer, but I don't want to interrupt your date."

"Nonsense. We'd love to have you." Kevin pushed to his feet and dusted off his pants. "Come and eat. It'll put the finishing touch on soothing out your nerves, and we can figure out what to do about Tom. Because if you ask me, he's not leaving without a fight."

There was nothing amazing in her fridge. She could stay here, scramble an egg, and call it a night. Or she could go out with the people who'd stepped in when she'd needed it. People she'd thought it would be nice to know better.

"If you're sure, okay. Let me wash my face."

17

Fury bubbled in Sean's veins as Larissa related the Friday night encounter with Tom. "Did he put his hands on you?"

"No. I'm okay. I am. See?" Larissa moved the camera from side to side, showing her full face and neck. "Renee and Kevin arrived just in time."

"Thank Jesus. And since? Has he bothered you again?"

"No. But I haven't been home. At dinner, we talked about it and Renee was emphatic I shouldn't go back to the apartment, because he'd come back. He pretty much said he would. So we swung by, I packed my things, and I'm staying with them."

"For how long? Will the school get you a different apartment? What about at work? Can he track you down there?" Sean paced his living room, squeezing his hands into fists and releasing them. There was nothing he could do to help. He was more than four thousand miles away. Even if he could hop a plane, it would take longer to get there than was useful.

"I don't know. I'm going to talk to them tomorrow. If they can't get me another place, I was thinking I'd just come home."

"Home?" He blinked. "You have six more weeks on your contract, don't you?"

"It's not a firm thing. People come and go. In the time I've been here, we've had teachers show up for a week, sometimes two, then move on. They're used to it when you're with the organization I used. It's not like the school system in the US." Larissa shrugged. "I don't think anyone would miss me. Turns out I'm not sure I want to stay. I overheard a conversation between two administrators last week and maybe things aren't as aboveboard with me working on this visa as I was told."

"What's that mean?"

"It sounded like the school routinely either pays an official to look the other way or apologizes and pays fines to make it all right rather than doing things correctly in the first place. Maybe it's okay, since the fees are taken care of in the long run, but I'm uncomfortable with it."

Sean nodded. "You should be. That's dishonest."

"It is, isn't it? I've been trying to convince myself I shouldn't worry about it—the teacher who's been there the longest says it's just the way things work in South America." Larissa frowned. "Even if it is, which I doubt, I don't think I can keep being part of it now that I know."

Sean smothered a smile. "You think you'll come home? Not find another teaching position in, I don't know, Uzbekistan?"

Larissa snickered. "I'm not sure Uzbekistan has ever been on my list, but I could check it out if you thought that was the way I should go."

"Not really."

"Me either. I miss home. I think that's the first time I've said it aloud. I had this map of my life planned out, you know? Then Tom sidelined things and I thought, okay, sure, this is better. When that imploded, I dragged things back onto my original map—and things came together so smoothly, I ignored the niggle in my belly that said it was the wrong move. I already emailed the private school where I used to teach to see if they have any positions opening up in the fall."

That was promising. "Where will you live?"

"I guess I'll throw myself on the mercy of Deidre until I can find something in Richmond. Do you think they'll have room? I know they were booking camps and retreats for the summer."

"I don't know, but you should definitely ask. If that doesn't work out, let me know. Maybe I can find someone at church who has a spare room you could snag for a while. If you come back here, won't Tom continue to be an issue? After all, he flew to Brazil." What did that say about the man? There was something going on, but what? At least Larissa didn't appear to have any interest in getting back together with him. If she came home, maybe they could make something real out of their relationship.

"At least in Richmond I have legal recourse. And friends. I've been in touch with some of the girls I used to hang with, trying to rebuild those friendships."

"How's it going?" He wanted her to have friends. She needed a support network—everyone needed one. It didn't have to be huge, but community was important on many levels.

"Slowly. Still, there's progress. Tom being out of the picture helps. None of them liked him. I wish they'd told me."

Sean should've said something as well. There'd been red flags—he'd ignored them. If he was going to insist he didn't do anything complicit in someone's sin, he ought to be brave enough to speak up when someone was getting ready to marry someone they shouldn't. "I think we all have regrets about that."

"Hey. It's okay. It wasn't your job. I saw them and ignored them. I seem to do a lot of that. I'm working on it. Look, I need to run. Renee and Kevin don't have a big place and they went out on the patio so we could have privacy, but I don't want them to feel like I'm kicking them out of their own home."

"Let me know your flight info if you end up heading back. I'll come get you at the airport."

"You don't have to do that. I can take a cab to my car."

"I know I don't have to. I want to. Where'd you end up parking?"

Larissa named one of the large churches in the area and he chuckled. He'd seen all sorts of vehicles parked in the far reaches of their parking lot.

"It seemed better than selling it. Though I had put it online for a while—no bites. People who look for cars on the Internet don't seem to want to pay what they're worth. I didn't need the money that badly. The church only asked for fifty bucks a month to store it and I figured that was easier than inconveniencing you. You're sure you don't mind picking me up?"

"Positive."

"Okay. I'll let you know one way or the other. If I don't come home early, does the airport ride offer stand?"

"Of course." His heart sank. Of course she might work it out to stay the rest of her three months. That was probably preferable, even if she was homesick. Homesickness could be temporary, brought on by Tom causing problems. She'd only ever been positive in their emails and video chats. "I haven't said it in a while, because I don't want to wig you out, but I love you."

Larissa smiled. "I know. I'll talk to you later. Gotta run."

Sean's screen blanked and he sighed. Would she ever love him back, or was he setting himself up for heartbreak?

SEAN SHIFTED his weight from side to side at the bottom of the escalators bringing passengers from the arrival terminal to baggage claim. He held a bouquet of roses and scanned the faces as they appeared. Larissa hadn't been in the first wave of passengers he'd been here for. That had caused a spear of panic through his heart. Had he missed her flight? A quick check of the monitors revealed that, no, he hadn't. So he waited. Now, a second set of people were making their way toward the baggage carousels. She had to be among them, didn't she?

Finally, his gaze landed on the face he'd drawn in his mind so many times over the past seven weeks. Sean grinned and waved. It took two heartbeats for her gaze to connect with his and her own smile to appear. When she reached the bottom of the stairs, she flung herself at him, her arms encircling his waist.

"Hi." Sean pressed a kiss to the top of Larissa's head and drew her out of the main traffic pattern. "How was your flight?"

"About like any airplane ride, I guess." She eased back and tilted her head back to meet his gaze again. "It's really good to see you."

Sean lowered his lips to hers, forcing himself to keep the contact light despite what he wanted to do. This wasn't the place. Nor was it the time. It would be a while before then. "What number did they say for your bags?"

"Three. I think they said three." Larissa frowned. "It was noisy and you know how those speakers are. They could be ordering takeout for all I could understand."

Sean laughed. "Let's try six. Sometimes the monitors actually work and we can double-check."

As they neared carousel three, the klaxon sounded and a red light started to strobe above the conveyor belt. With several loud clunking noises, the belt began to move.

"That's promising. At least we know someone's luggage is coming out at three." Sean gave her the bouquet, took Larissa's hand, and tugged, navigating them around a clump of passengers standing directly where the bags first appeared. "Let's move down here—it's less crowded."

"Some of these people look familiar."

Then they were probably in the right spot.

"I was frustrated, at first, that we had to go through Miami since there are some international flights direct to Richmond. But it's nice to have customs out of the way and not have to drag my suitcases anywhere but to the car now. It took so long to clear through customs I nearly missed my flight though—it was good our flight from Brazil left early."

"Early? I didn't think they could do that."

"Apparently they can. I guess everyone was checked in and onboard. Whatever the reason, I'm grateful. Customs took forever—it seemed like no one on my flight spoke English or filled the forms out properly?" Larissa sighed. "At least it wasn't as bad as the school exit interview."

"Did the school give you a hard time?"

"Not really. My company already has a replacement on the way, so they're not losing an instructor for long. And I guess the students are used to it. No, their big concern was that Tom went back to the apartment and caused another ruckus. Now they might not get to lease that space again. I guess the neighbors complained and called the police. I'm not sure Tom is welcome in Brazil anymore."

Sean fought a laugh. Served the man right. It was impossible to guess what the guy had been thinking. Did he expect Larissa to throw herself at him? And just forget he'd left her at the altar? Some women might, but it was the exception not the rule. "You think he's back here already?"

"Probably."

"What are you going to do?"

"Not think about it until he's a problem. Hopefully he's smart enough to not get involved with the police here, too. Oh, that one's mine." She pointed to a large black bag with a pink unicorn embroidered on the side.

"Unicorns, huh?" Sean lugged the bag off the carousel. "Unicorns full of bricks."

"It's unique. No one's taken it by accident yet."

He laughed. "I guess not. Are they all unicorns?"

She nodded. "Only two more."

Their conversation was light as they got the bags out to the car and navigated out of the airport.

"Do you want to grab some dinner?" He hoped she'd say yes. His stomach was grumbling and it was likely to reach an embarrassing noise level before much longer.

"If you want. I never seem to get hungry when I fly. I guess that's good now that everything seems to cost extra. But it's supper time, so I can have a salad or something."

"I could just hit a drive though after I drop you off at your car." The half-formed vision of a romantic, candlelit dinner with Larissa fizzled away. It was unrealistic anyway. She was probably exhausted after her day in the air—and the days leading up to leaving. There was time. He wasn't in a rush.

Sean would keep repeating that to himself. Maybe he'd get to a point where he believed it.

Larissa reached over and rested her hand on his arm. "Did I mention I'm really glad to see you?"

Heat spread out from her fingertips, and he curled his fingers over hers. It wasn't more than twenty minutes in normal traffic to where she'd parked her car, and he had no reason to offer to follow her to Peacock Hill. Anyway, appointments in Richmond tomorrow meant he couldn't.

For the first time in his life, he wished for heavy traffic.

18

L arissa squeezed her eyes shut against the sunlight streaming through the windows. She rolled to her stomach and tugged the pillow over her head. There was no possible way it was already time to get up. And yet ... she peeked out into the room and scanned the walls for a clock. Nothing but the curving stones of the tower. She slipped an arm from under the sheet and patted around on the nightstand until she found her phone and checked the time.

After ten?

She pushed herself up to sag against the tufted headboard. How did it get so late in the day? It was one in the afternoon in San Paulo time, the time her body clock should be used to. Apparently, five nights of tossing, turning, and jolting awake at every little noise finally caught up with her.

She glanced around the room. Azure had taken the odd stone tower that speared up above the tree line and turned it into something magical. Larissa had scarcely believed it was possible when Azure had outlined her plans. And didn't that seem like a lifetime ago? But the woman knew what she was doing. Must be her artist's eye.

There were three floors. The bedroom was at the top, with the bed set up to showcase the amazing vista. She threw off her blankets—it was warm up here. The tower didn't have air conditioning, unlike the main house. A humid breeze wafted from the fan suspended from the conical ceiling above her, and the windows were open. What was the plan for heating the space in the winter? It wasn't as if there was a way to put in fireplaces. Electric heaters, maybe?

They'd sectioned off a small portion of the room for a shower and toilet. There was another bathroom on the middle floor, although that was only a half bath. The main floor held the kitchen and a small eating space. Azure had insisted no one wanted to carry groceries up even one flight of the stairs curving around the circular wall.

Larissa tossed her legs over the edge of the bed and curled her toes in the thick throw rug. The colorful swirls reminded her of the wind blowing leaves on a blustery fall day. She hummed under her breath as she brushed her teeth and dressed. Even if it was practically lunchtime, she needed coffee.

She paused on the middle floor to appreciate the cozy sitting area Azure had created. This was going to be a stellar vacation rental when they decided to put it online. Larissa had been skeptical—the tower was weird when she considered how different it was from the rest of Peacock Hill—but this was amazing.

On the ground floor, she dropped a coffee pod into the machine, lined up a mug, and hit brew. There was no denying the machine was convenient, but the waste bothered her. But there wasn't another option. Maybe she'd suggest they get a small drip coffee maker. Or one of the single-cup pourover kinds. Or a French Press.

There was a light tap at the door.

Larissa couldn't make out who was on the other side of the

warm wood door with the curved arch and wavy glass window. She pulled it open.

Azure, eyes dancing with laughter, lifted a hand in greeting. "Morning, sleepyhead."

"Morning. Come on in." The coffee beeped its completion and Larissa gestured at the machine. "Want some?"

Azure considered a moment before nodding. "Why not? If I'm up all night, I'll blame you. Maybe I'll get some painting done."

Larissa carried her mug to the little table and sat. "Sounds fair. Make it a good picture though? I don't want to be responsible for something awful."

Azure laughed and dropped a pod in the machine. "So? How was it? You're our first resident and we're all dying to know. I had to do some fast talking to keep everyone from descending to grill you. Or I would have if the current retreat wasn't full of obnoxious teenagers who are driving Deidre and Claire mad. Honestly, if I were them, I'd be rethinking youth groups. They need a minimum age. Or a higher counselor-to-student ratio. Something."

"I'll be sure to steer clear of the house. When do they leave?"

"Saturday at ten. Only two more days, thank the Lord. And I don't mean that facetiously. I am honestly thanking Jesus—and I'm not even here most of the day since I'm down at the garage helping Matt."

"But not today."

"Well, I was there but decided to take an early lunch and see if you were up so I could find out about the tower. Does it work?"

Larissa grinned. "It does. It's amazing. The bed is super comfortable, although I don't understand how you got it up there."

"With a lot of grumbling from the guys and some creative

wiggling. Thankfully mattresses are flexible. Bathroom isn't too small?"

"I showered last night and it was fine. I mean, it's not a spa, but it gets you clean and you're not rapping elbows on walls. It should be good for anyone who isn't crazy tall."

"I should see if Jeremiah will take a shower in there. He's tall. Everything else though? It was good?"

"You have a winner. Getting luggage upstairs is a pain, but in the overall scheme, that's not a big deal. You only have to lug it up and down once. If they're cooking in, not having to drag groceries upstairs is smart. And the sitting level? It's a dream. You did a great job."

Pink flushed Azure's cheeks. "Excellent. I'm glad you like it. I've been second-guessing everything in here. Deidre gave me carte blanche and . . . that's a lot of pressure, you know? It's completely different from the retreat-slash-camp-slash-conference center thing she's got going on at the main house. I'm not sure she's convinced vacationing couples meshes with that business model—maybe it doesn't—but it was a crime to let this thing sit empty when it was in such good shape and only needed a little creative love to get it fixed up."

Would she vacation in the tower at Peacock Hill? She would. It was a romantic spot—the bedroom would be an amazing honeymoon destination. Heat flooded her face as an image of Sean, sans shirt, flitted through her mind. She'd seen his chest only once—when she'd stopped by on her way to Brazil—and that was just a fleeting glimpse. While he wasn't one of those gym-rat-Adonis types, he'd made her mouth water. But he did that in a suit, like he wore for weddings. Or jeans. Or shorts. Honestly, chemistry with the man was no problem.

"Did I lose you?" Azure brought her coffee over and sat across from Larissa. "Was it at least a good daydream?"

She had to resemble a tomato at this point. Larissa took a

long drink from her mug. "Just thinking about vacation prospects. What would you recommend as attractions in the area? You're not exactly close to anything."

"I was thinking we'd sell it as secluded. Removed from the hustle and bustle, but still within striking distance. That sort of thing. I mean, Monticello isn't that far—an hour maybe? Go the other direction and you've got the Frontier Culture Museum. Plus there are ample hiking trails right here—we're on the doorstep of the Shenandoah National Forest." Azure shrugged. "There's plenty to do."

If that was the sort of vacation people were in the market for, Azure was probably right. And if it was primarily honeymooners, well, they weren't as likely to be leaving the tower all that much anyway. "Are you thinking of some sort of food package? What if people don't want to cook?"

"I guess in that case, they'll be spending a lot of time driving to eat at the restaurants in town. Maybe I'll talk to Deidre about some sort of light breakfast options. We could stock bagels or waffles in the freezer. It's a thought." Azure dug her phone out of her pocket and jotted some notes. "This is why it's good to have someone test run the place before we get the official listing set up."

"Happy to help. Grateful, actually. I could probably talk some friends in Richmond into letting me couch surf, but—"

"Ugh. That's the worst. Even when I spent all my time moving from place to place, I had my own bed. Couches—and being right in the middle of people's living space? Not a long-term solution at all. You're thinking you'll head back to Richmond? Stay in the area?"

"That's the plan. I'm hoping to hear about a full-time teaching position at the school where I used to work. Maybe as early as next week. The principal was positive when we spoke. I've been, well, praying about it actually. A lot." Larissa ran her finger around the edge of her mug. "I've been a Christian since I was young, but praying was never something that was part of my day-to-day life. I mean, sure, bless the food and before bed—that sort of thing—but to think God cared about things like this? My job? Who I married? Sure He cared, but on a macro level—like He wanted generic good things for me, but it was up to me to make that happen. Now I'm starting to see that it's different. He cares about me—not just as His creation, but as Larissa. And that's weird."

"No. It's not weird. It's good. I think it's something everyone struggles with, one way or another. Maybe those of us who are independent and capable a bit more than others."

Larissa snickered.

"So. Teaching job in Richmond. I'll pray you'll see God's leading. Do you have a backup plan?"

"No. I guess I can keep stringing together ESL online. Maybe in person, too. There are options to look into. I felt I should wait and see what happened with the school first. It's what my heart wants. I loved it there."

Azure frowned. "Then why'd you leave?"

"Tom. Teaching took up too much time, and I was always beat on Friday nights, which interfered with his see-and-be-seen schedule." Larissa drained her mug and glanced at the coffee machine. A second cup was a terrible idea this late in the day, but boy she wanted one. "If I'd been paying attention, maybe I would have figured out what a bad plan staying with him was."

"Learning to hear the Holy Spirit is an ongoing thing."

The Holy Spirit. Kevin and Renee had talked about Him a lot the few days she'd stayed with them in Brazil. It was something else she'd known about but never internalized. Salvation, sure, she had that covered, but had she ever really lived for Jesus the way He wanted? Had she let Him work on transforming her into His image? If she had to ask, the answer was probably no.

Well, that was changing. Starting now. "I guess that's comforting to know. But anyway, yes, I'd appreciate you praying with me for guidance. If that isn't weird."

"Not weird at all. Can I tell the others?"

"Why not? Isn't there something about that in the Bible?"

"Yeah, in James I think. Keep us posted?" Azure stood and carried her mug to the sink. She rinsed it and set it in the top rack of the small dishwasher.

"Sure. When were you planning to try and list the tower? I can speed up my search for something in Richmond."

"There's no rush. Maybe after Matt and I get back from our honeymoon in September. Deidre and Claire are slammed with stuff at the house right now and don't want to add to that until things start tapering off. As far as we're concerned, you're welcome to stay until after the wedding. You're coming to that, right?"

"Your wedding?"

Azure nodded. "Labor Day. Sean'll be there."

"I imagine he'll be a bit busy."

"Still. Any chance to see him all dressed up, right?"

Man, she wanted another cup of coffee. Larissa rose and filled her mug with water at the sink. The cool liquid soothed her burning throat. "He does look nice in a suit."

Azure snorted. "Nice? Come on."

"Aren't you engaged?"

"Sure. But not blind."

"I'll talk to him about it and see if he minds me being there. I don't want to be a distraction."

"All right. So . . . does that mean you're an item?"

Was that all that was? Fishing to see her relationship status? "We haven't talked about it specifically."

"What do you mean? He went on and on about how much he missed you and looked forward to your weekly chats. I thought for sure . . . and from the look in your eye, it's not any of my business."

"It's not that. Or not exactly." Larissa finished her water and set her mug in the sink. She could deal with it later. "I—you're in love with Matt, right?"

"Yeah. I'll leave off the 'duh'."

"Thanks. Sean says he loves me and—"

"Wait. Why can't he just love you? I mean it's great that he said it to you. But the way you say it makes it sound like you don't believe it. Why wouldn't you?"

Larissa returned to her seat and leaned forward. "Tom said he loved me, and look how that turned out. What if I'm not someone who can actually be loved?"

"Everyone can be loved." Azure drummed her fingers on the table. "Matt and I have been arguing a lot about what Bible readings we want at our wedding. He's adamant we read First Corinthians chapter thirteen. I think it's hokey. At the same time? It's a great definition of love. Patient. Kind. All those things. Is Sean those things to you?"

Was he? Of course he was. She'd have to go back and reread the passage, but patient and kind? Yeah, that was Sean to a T. "I don't think Tom and I had that one—well, we hadn't planned to. We didn't end up using any of them. I guess I should go back and read it. And at least Matt's involved. If he really wants it, why not let him? You can have more than one reading."

Azure laughed. "That's a point. I'll think about it. It just makes me squirmy."

"Why?"

"I don't know. It's a tall order, a big standard, however you want to look at it. Reading it at the wedding makes it seem like a rule. I mean, if I lose my patience with Matt, do I suddenly not love him?"

"Gonna go with no on that. But maybe if it starts to be a

habit you have things to think about and work on. Don't think rule, think . . . yardstick."

"Look at you, smarty. All right, fine. I'll let Matt have his First Corinthians. But I still want Song of Solomon chapter two."

"Figure out a way to have both. Pretty sure the two of you are flexible enough to find a compromise." What Larissa had seen of their relationship told her they were committed to doing that. Having a man who was invested enough to have opinions and push for them? That was priceless. She'd thought it was a positive that Tom had left so much of the wedding to her. Now she was beginning to think it was that he hadn't cared enough to participate. If he'd shown up, she would have married him. How long would he have stayed?

19

Sean sat on the couch and looked around the middle floor of the Peacock Hill tower. "This is nicer than I thought it'd be."

"Right? I'm enjoying staying here. If I could make it a permanent solution, I totally would. Except for the going insane after two weeks thing. That's definitely a downside."

Sean snickered. "You, too? I love to come out here and visit, but I couldn't live here. It's such a small town. Give me the city any day. Or at least the suburbs."

"Speaking of suburbs—I have an interview at the school on Tuesday. The principal assures me—well, as much as he legally can—that it's a formality, but I'm still nervous. I could probably make the drive Tuesday morning, but I was thinking maybe I could crash on your couch tomorrow night instead."

Sean flinched. That was asking for temptation. Obviously she wasn't comfortable enough with her renewed friendships with girlfriends to ask them. So she must be in a spot, but . . . it was a bad plan.

"Or not. I just—I'll see if I can find a cheap hotel."

"No. That's dumb. Stay at my place. I'll crash on Topher's couch."

"Shouldn't you ask him first? I don't mean to kick you out of your house. I just thought it wouldn't be a problem to crash."

"Larissa." Sean reached for her hand and gently squeezed her fingers. "I can only be so noble. I love you. I want to spend the rest of my life with you. If you were asleep on my couch, it'd be entirely too easy to start making justifications about legalities."

"Oh." She blushed a dark pink. "I didn't think about that. I should have. Probably. I used to bunk over in Tom's guest room every now and then. Nothing ever happened—I was always clear nothing would—was that wrong?"

"I can't answer that. That's between you and Jesus. I'm glad things never went too far, but there's an appearance element as well. As vocal as I am about premarital sex, I can't afford to skirt the line. And I don't want to put myself in that situation. Honestly? I'm not sure we should hang out in here alone much longer. Want to go for a walk around the grounds?"

Larissa blinked. "Sure. How hot is it?"

"It's July. It's hot and muggy. But there's a breeze and we're in the foothills, not the city. It shouldn't be too bad. Not much worse than in here." Sean shrugged. "I'm not sure how you'd put A/C in a building like this, but I wish it had been possible."

She chuckled. "That would make it perfect. The fans help, and the windows. It's not awful."

"You're sleeping okay?" Sean stood and held out his hand. He gave her a light tug and helped her to her feet.

"Better than I have in a week. Maybe two. Some of that is being home." She slipped her feet into sandals and headed toward the stairs. "I'm glad you could come out today. I know Sundays are your only real day off."

Sean followed her down the stairs, through the kitchen, and

out into the clearing surrounding the tower. The breeze made it much nicer, although the afternoon sun pounding down on them was strong. "I wanted to see you. And since you're coming up tomorrow, can we plan on dinner? And maybe something after your interview? Now that you're close, I want to spend as much time with you as you can manage."

Larissa stopped, her gaze zipping to and holding his. She stepped closer and slid her arms around his waist. "I'll make as much time as you can spare. I don't want you to put your life on hold for me. I know you're busy."

"Things are lightening up. In fact, I don't have a wedding this weekend. What would you say to a real Saturday night date?"

"Aw, man. Really? I didn't think that was a possibility. They're having a get-together here, and I said I'd come. Do you want to join us? It's mostly couples, except Claire and Danny." Larissa winced. "I don't think Danny's going to bring his girlfriend. Hopefully he's not that cruel."

Sean pressed his lips to hers in a brief kiss before stepping back and taking her hand. "Let's walk by the lake."

"I've only seen Claire with Danny a handful of times, and even I've picked up on the fact that she likes him. How does Danny not get it?"

He drew them toward a shady path, the temperature easing off by a few degrees as they wandered deeper into the leafy cover. "Why hasn't someone said something to him?"

"Because that's just weird. It's between the two of them to figure out."

"So she should say something."

Larissa snorted. "Do you understand women at all? Most of us don't want to be the one to make the first move."

"I thought it was the age of female empowerment."

She stopped and crossed her arms. "That doesn't mean women need to take the lead in stuff like this."

Didn't it? "I always thought that was exactly what it meant. So if it's not that, what is it?"

"Equal pay for equal work. That sort of thing."

He nodded. It seemed like the safest response. Sean wasn't convinced the equal pay thing hadn't been going on for quite some time, but he also wasn't dumb enough to get into an argument about it.

Larissa didn't let it go. "You're not one of those 'weaker sex' people, are you?"

"No. But I do believe God gave everyone different talents, and that we should play to those. Use what we have and who we are for God's glory, not try to be something or someone we aren't."

After a moment, Larissa nodded. "Okay. I can agree with that. I have a lot of experience with trying to be something I'm not. It's not as rewarding as it seems like it should be."

They walked a few minutes in the quiet of the summer afternoon. He liked the feel of her hand in his. Having her at his side made him complete, like he'd found something he didn't even know he'd been missing. Would she ever feel the same way?

They came to a bench nestled in a copse of trees. Larissa ran her hand along the back of it and angled her head so she could catch his gaze. "You want to sit for a few minutes?"

"Sure." Sean sat and rested his arm along the back of the bench, curling his hand around her shoulder. "This is nice."

"I love you."

He blinked and shifted so he could see her face.

She nodded. "I had a good conversation with Azure the other day, and I realized I needed to stop second-guessing your feelings for me and mine for you."

"Remind me to do something special for Matt and Azure's wedding as a thank you."

Larissa laughed, but ended with a sigh.

"What's that for?"

"I'm trying—hard—to stop swearing. Again. I've been thinking about what you said about sin—how we're all sinners, even Christians—and that there isn't one kind of sin that's worse than others. I know God doesn't want me to swear, but it's a bigger challenge than I realized. And I have to keep reminding myself that my justifications aren't valid."

"What do you mean?" How had they gone from her finally telling him she loved him to this? He could—barely—follow the train of thought. Was it all part and parcel of her trying to listen more to God and walk more fully with Him? He was all for that. For anyone. He wanted more of that for himself.

"I'm back to that same justification we used to laugh about in high school. How Jesus talks about how thinking a bad name at someone it's the same as murdering them. So if I think the word, what's the difference if I say it? But I know that's faulty logic."

"Ideally, you'd want to get to not even thinking the word."

She smiled and nuzzled her head into his shoulder. "Ideally, yes. Someday, I hope. But I have to start somewhere."

"True. How are you doing it? Swear jar?"

"I thought about it. But when it's just me, it's not super motivating."

He could join in—toss in a quarter every time he wanted to swear at someone. With the handful of brides still on his plate, there were definite temptations. Sean opened his mouth to offer that, but Larissa spoke again.

"So I was wondering if you'd keep track of it for me."

"I'd love that—but I'm only here when I can swing a Sunday afternoon. At least for now. It'll be easier when we're at least living in the same city."

"Right. Which is why I was digging around online—there's an app."

Sean snickered. "Of course there is."

Larissa slipped her phone out of her pocket and tapped the screen. "See? It's easy—I tap here when I swear and it adds a quarter. You can join my virtual jar, and that'll keep me motivated."

"And honest?"

"That I can promise. The girls here—they're on me if I'm around them. In some ways it's been helpful, because I'm getting more aware of it." Larissa shrugged. "It's baby steps, but maybe the money can be earmarked for our wedding or something."

Sean's breath caught and his heart hammered in his chest. Having her say she loved him had been enough to keep him going for weeks—maybe months—but the hint at a future? He lowered his forehead to hers. "That sounds like an amazing idea."

"I'll text y—" He stopped her words with a kiss and let the sounds of a summer afternoon fade as he lost himself in it.

"LOOKED like you two were having a nice afternoon out by the lake." Deidre grinned and set the bowl she was carrying on the long table in the more formal dining area. When Sean had first come to look at Peacock Hill as a potential wedding venue, she'd told him the table and chairs were made by her now-husband Jeremiah. The man had talent. Even better was knowing the residents used the space rather than leaving it to gleam and gather dust.

"We did. Still hot and muggy though." Sean aimed for casual. If she'd seen them kissing, well, there was nothing to be embarrassed by. He'd seen more inappropriate contact from couples he'd planned weddings for. During their weddings.

"Where'd Larissa go?"

"She said she wanted a shower before dinner. Like I said, hot

and muggy. I told her it was fine, but there was no dissuading her."
He was working on not taking it personally. He only had maybe an
hour after they ate with the gang before he had to head back to Richmond. Sure, they'd see each other again tomorrow evening when
she came out for her interview, but now that she was back in the
country, he ached to spend as much time with her as he could swing.

Deidre nodded. "Today was kind of gross. Still better than in
the city, I imagine. Can you go in and grab the dish of green
beans?"

"Sure." Sean pushed the swinging kitchen door and sniffed
the homey scents filling the smaller room.

Jeremiah glanced up from the stove with a nod. "Sean. Glad
you two could join us for dinner. Larissa keeps to herself a lot."

"Not in the worried you'll someday find she's a serial killer
way, right?"

Jeremiah laughed. "No. She just doesn't come down from the
tower much. I guess it suits her needs too well."

"It seems to. It's a great space. Let me know when you're
ready to start renting it. I suspect I can add it to a first night
package for weddings with very little complaint. Especially if I
work with the caterer to stock the kitchen."

"You think so?"

"Absolutely." Sean eyed the dishes on the counter. "Deidre
sent me for green beans."

"Oh, sure." Jeremiah grabbed the correct bowl and thrust it
at Sean. "Would you let her know we're about ten minutes out
on the lasagna?"

"Sure." He carried the bowl back into the dining room and
relayed the message. It was nice to see a couple who worked so
well together—even with something as simple and pedestrian as
making dinner for friends. Would he and Larissa settle into that
same sort of comfortable rhythm? He hoped so. For all Jeremiah

and Deidre had ease, there were still visible sparks. That was good to see as well. Of course, for all their various faults—and who didn't have those?—his parents had been married coming up on thirty-five years now and *they* still showed sparks if people knew where to look. Marriage—having an outlet for those sparks—was a good thing.

"You might as well get comfortable. I texted everyone the ten minute warning, but it's likely to be twenty before we're sitting down. Matt and Azure went to Jeremiah's house to look around. They're on the way back, but it's a little more than ten to get here. Claire is down in her apartment and honestly? I don't think she'd come if she could figure out how to get out of it without making me angry." Deidre frowned. "I don't know what to do about that. I'd like to kick Danny, but Jeremiah says that won't solve anything."

"Don't look at me. I was telling Larissa earlier that I thought someone ought to explain things to Danny. She said that was the worst possible solution." Sean turned at the sound of a car on the gravel driveway. "Here's someone."

"Maybe Danny. I don't recognize the car, though." Deidre peered around Sean, her frown deepening. "No, that's not Danny. I don't know who that is."

Sean glanced, then looked more closely, his stomach tightening as realization dawned. "Can you call Larissa? Tell her to stay at the tower and lock the door."

"I can. But wh—" She broke off as the man began pounding on the front door.

"Larissa! Get down here now, Larissa! We have things to talk about."

"I'll handle him." Sean took a deep breath. "You tell Larissa to stay away."

Deidre nodded and scurried into the kitchen.

"Larissa!" The pounding increased in volume. The door shook with each bang.

Sean wrenched open the door, stepping back so he didn't get hit. "Tom."

"What are you doing here? Where's Larissa?" Tom tried to step in.

Sean put up his hand. "Hold up. Let's step outside and chat for a minute."

"I don't have anything to say to you." Tom raised his voice. "Larissa!"

"You're going to want to stop now, Tom." Sean edged out the door and pulled it shut behind him, easing Tom backward before the bigger man realized what was happening. Sean kept his voice low and friendly, his time-honored method of dealing with overexcited wedding guests. There was a hint of steel in the words that most people missed the first time. "What brings you out to Peacock Hill this evening?"

"That's between me and my fiancée."

"And who's that?"

"Don't be an idiot. You're planning our wedding. Or you will be. Again. I realize there's a little hiccup we need to get through, but as soon as Larissa and I talk, I know she'll come around."

Was the man stupid? Or was he under the influence of mind-altering substances? "I heard you tried to talk to her in Brazil, and she made it clear she wasn't interested."

Tom glowered. "I might have gone about that the wrong way. But she's mine. She has no right to tell me no."

"Again, I'm not completely sure you're up to date, Tom. You didn't show up at your wedding. She returned your ring and has made it clear she's not interested in continuing a relationship with you. She's no longer yours in any way, and I understand she has no interest in taking you back."

"You don't get to talk to me like that." Tom's hand bunched

into a fist. "This is between me and Larissa. If I were you, I'd get out of the way."

"I'm afraid I can't do that." Sean fought a sigh as Tom stepped forward. So much for reasonable. "You're going to want to back up."

"Or what?"

"Or someone inside will call the police. I imagine the police here can talk to the police in Brazil easily enough, should that become necessary. Don't do this, Tom. You made a choice. Now you need to live with it."

"I need a wife—or at least a fiancée. We don't even have to get married if she's not sure about that anymore. We could live together, unless she's going to stay a puritan. How was I supposed to know I was only eligible for partner because of her?" Tom's voice held a hint of a whine.

Pieces started to fall into place. When he'd been helping Larissa with the wedding planning, her usual excuse for Tom missing the appointment was how busy he was at work because he was in line for a partnership. The old family law firm must still hold to some of the more conservative—maybe even outdated—ideas when it came to partnerships. "You lost the promotion?"

"I can still have it. I just need Larissa to take me back." Sweat beaded Tom's forehead. "I need that raise. Do you have any idea what kind of expenses I have?"

Tom must have considered the promotion a done deal if he'd already started spending like he had the salary. "She doesn't want to see you, Tom."

"She will. If I can get to her, I can make her see."

"No, Tom, you can't." Larissa touched Sean's shoulder as she came onto the porch. "You need to go."

"This is all a big misunderstanding, honey. Come on. I need a chance to explain."

"I heard enough when you explained to Sean. I'm not interested in helping you become partner. Did you ever love me?"

Sean glanced over, his heart breaking at the tears brimming in her eyes. He took her hand and squeezed.

Tom's gaze darted to Sean and Larissa's joined hands and his expression hardened. "I knew it. I *knew* you were cheating. Why do you think I didn't show up?"

Larissa sighed. "If you need to believe that to get through the day, go ahead. You know better. Now, since you're not listening when Sean says it, let me reiterate: you need to go, Tom. There's nothing for you here."

Fists balled at his side, Tom glared at each of them before stalking to his car. He revved the engine before peeling down the driveway. A gray blur darted across the car's path. Larissa drew in a fast breath. "Was that a squirrel?"

Sean was halfway down the stairs. "Too big for that. Get some towels."

He jogged down the driveway to the motionless gray lump. Definitely not a squirrel, though it wasn't much bigger. A kitten? He squatted beside the animal and chewed his lip. All things considered, the cat had fared better than expected. One leg was bleeding, but nothing else seemed visibly wrong.

"Here. Dishtowels. It's the best I could find." Larissa dropped to her knees beside Sean. "Is it still alive?"

"I think so. If you watch carefully, its chest is moving." Sean stared at the towels and the kitten. "Go see if they have an empty box. And ask where the nearest vet is."

Larissa nodded and disappeared.

Sean stroked a finger gently down the curve of the kitten's back before wrapping the damaged leg in the towels. The cat gave a strangled *mew* but didn't fight him. The silent litany of prayers for safety he'd kept up while talking to Tom shifted to the poor cat.

Larissa returned with a box. Deidre and Jeremiah followed close behind.

"Oh. Poor baby. I've seen it around the past couple of weeks and have been trying to entice her into the house." Deidre wrapped her arm around Jeremiah's waist. "Will it be okay?"

Gingerly, Sean lifted the cat into the box. "I don't know, but I'll see what can be done. The vet?"

"Check your phone. I texted the address." Jeremiah shook his head. "It's about twenty minutes away."

"Then I guess I'd better get started. You stay here and eat." He ran a hand down Larissa's arm. "I'd like you to be around people."

"You're people." Larissa frowned.

"Please? For me?" Sean huffed out a breath. "I know that's not fair. I'm sorry. But with Tom—and I don't know how long this will take."

Larissa looked like she was going to argue, then her shoulders sagged. "Okay. On record, I don't prefer it, but I appreciate the inclination to protect me."

"Thanks." The hot ball in his chest loosened a fraction. He glanced at Jeremiah. "Make sure everything is locked."

Jeremiah nodded. "You know it. Let us know how the cat is."

Sean brushed his lips across Larissa's before carefully picking up the box with the cat in it and heading toward his car. Today had been a strange, strange day.

20

Larissa left the school building with a spring in her step. Her interview couldn't have gone better. If she didn't get an offer, well, God must have something else for her. But she couldn't imagine not getting the offer.

As she got to her car, her phone started to ring. Her heart gave a little jolt as Sean's name flashed on the screen. "Hey. I planned to call you in a minute so we didn't have to wait through the weird Bluetooth connection thing."

Sean laughed. "How'd it go?"

"It was great. I think I'm going to get an offer. Maybe even today. The principal has to run it past the board, but I've worked here before, so they all know me. To my knowledge, there's nothing there that would turn someone off." Larissa paused and frowned. She'd left under good circumstances—she'd even been asked to stay, although she'd said no. It wasn't as if she'd left in the middle of the term. She hadn't burned bridges.

"And the job?"

"Not exactly what I thought, but maybe better. It's a fourth-grade position. Like all of fourth grade, not just English. So that's a little scary, but I have my elementary education certificate and I know how—I just never have. But they have curriculum and there are two fourth-grade classes, so the other teacher said he'd help."

"He?"

She chuckled and started the car. When she was sure the phone had connected through the stereo, she spoke, "Yes, he. Married he. Probably my dad's age married he."

"Okay. That's better."

"You're not really jealous, are you?" Jealousy would not be a good sign. She was going to have to work with men. And Sean worked primarily with women.

"No, I'm kidding. Promise." He paused. When she stayed quiet, he added, "I promise it was a joke. The reality is, when people find out I'm a wedding-slash-event planner, they all assume I'm gay and haven't realized it."

Larissa snorted.

"Don't laugh. Didn't you say Tom thought that? It happens more than you'd expect."

"We'll just have to have a lot of kids then." She pressed her lips together. Was that too much? They hadn't really talked kids. She knew he wanted some, generically, but there was so much they still needed to talk through before they could plan a life together. She wasn't letting him take a pass on the conversation either. Not like she had with Tom. That was one—of many— lessons she'd learned.

"Suits me. I've always wanted four. Are you heading back to my place or did you want to meet up at a restaurant? I know you need to get back to Peacock Hill."

She didn't need to get back there. Not really. She'd taken the day off from her online teaching since she hadn't known how long the interview would take. She did feel a little guilty leaving Deidre in charge of Misty Kitty. The poor thing needed extra care as she learned to manage without one of her legs. The vet said she'd be fine, but still. "I can be flexible. Tell me what you'd prefer."

"Why don't you head to my place? I'll be there in about ten and we can figure out what's next."

"Okay. See you soon." Larissa paused. "I love you."

"I love you, too." She could hear the smile in his voice and it warmed her inside. She disconnected the call and pointed her car toward Sean's. She'd loaded her overnight bag in the car when she left that morning. She hadn't wanted him to get the wrong idea—or worry that she was going to take up his space.

Figure out what's next. What had he meant by that? Her thoughts skipped around as she tried to call up how his voice sounded. Did he mean a late lunch? Or was it more than that?

Her heart pounded. She wasn't ready for more. Not yet. What was next? She needed a job. That was the first thing. Then an apartment. In fact, she was going to stop at the grocery store near Sean's and grab some of the apartment hunter books they had in stacks by the door. It was past time she started looking for a new place. Sure, she'd do a lot of looking online, but the books were a good way to narrow the search by section of the city. She could check on the handful she'd been looking at in the spring, as well. Maybe there were vacancies now. But she needed to lock something in before mid-August when the local colleges started back and kids who didn't want to stay on campus absorbed all the empty units.

Or maybe she could rent a house. There were good neighborhoods near the school. There might be some rentals available. But what would the price be for that? She needed a real estate agent. Or an app. Start with an app, then call an agent if needed.

She let out a breath. There was no need to panic. He probably just meant lunch, and the two of them could laugh about her mini-anxiety attack while they ate.

After a quick stop to grab the apartment hunter magazines and download a real estate app on her phone, Larissa finally pulled into a visitor parking space at Sean's. His car was already in the spot closest to his door. That wasn't ten minutes. Was it? She glanced at the dashboard clock and groaned. Closer to twenty.

Larissa jogged up the steps and knocked on Sean's door. She clutched the booklets to her chest and waited.

"There you are. I was worried you got lost." Sean grinned and pushed the door open further, stepping back to give her room. His hair gleamed wet in the sun. "Come on in."

He smelled like soap and man. She had to fight the urge to stop, wrap her arms around him, and just sniff. "Sorry. Made a stop on the way."

"Apartment books. Good call. You're confident about the job?"

He hadn't even blinked. See? She'd way overreacted. "I am. But more than that? I'm sure it's time to get a place back in Richmond. If this job doesn't work out, here is where I'm going to find one that does. Worst case scenario, I can substitute and still do the online thing."

"That's my girl. I'll enjoy having you closer. Although right now, with the Tom situation, I feel better that you're a bit of a drive away if he wants to harass you."

She nodded. "He tried to call."

Sean frowned.

"I know. I thought I had his number blocked—I do now. And I called his boss. Mr. Evans is a nice older man, like a grandpa. We hit it off pretty well at the events I used to go to with Tom. I explained the situation and he assured me he'd take care of it."

Sean winced. "I hope that doesn't make Tom even more unhinged."

"I don't think it will." She hadn't even considered that it

could. Would she ever get to the place where she thought—and prayed—about things before she did them? Of course she would. She was making progress. Look at her job hunt. And the house hunt would be the same thing. She'd do better. "Sorry."

"What for? You did what you thought made sense. We'll both pray it works. It's probably fine. So what's next?"

Larissa swallowed the lump in her throat. He meant lunch. Or something normal. Even as she reminded herself of that, she blurted, "I can't marry you yet."

Sean's mouth twitched—but whether it was a smile or a frown, Larissa couldn't decide. "Let's sit down."

Larissa's mouth went dry. "I'm sorry. I just—you said that before? On the phone? And I started thinking. Panicking. I thought I had it under control and then *wham!* It was all back. Please don't be angry. Or dump me. I love you."

This time, Sean did smile. He tugged her down on the couch beside him and pulled her snug to his side. "It happens. I meant lunch. Maybe getting you to spend the afternoon and heading over to Maymont to wander through the gardens for an hour or something."

She turned her burning face into his shoulder. "I know I'm obsessing and stupid."

"Stop. I haven't pushed about the future—our future— because I know you need time. We need time. In some ways, we've known each other for almost two years. But for more than half of that, you were engaged to someone else. It's no secret I want to marry you, but I'm not going to ask until I know you're ready."

"What if it takes a long time?" Her voice was caught somewhere between a whisper and a croak. How was she even supposed to know she was ready? She'd thought she was ready to marry Tom, and that had been a disaster.

"Why don't we just keep praying about it and see what

happens?" Sean pressed a tender kiss to her lips. "I love you. I don't want that to panic you."

"Okay." She should say more. Something. But there were no words in her brain.

"So. Lunch? The gardens? Or did you want to get back to Peacock Hill?"

Fatigue shot through her. What did she expect with the emotional ups and downs she'd put herself through in the last hour? Still, sitting in the car alone—even with the radio cranked to drown out her singing—didn't appeal. Not yet. She wanted more Sean. "You know what? Lunch and the gardens sounds perfect."

Sean grinned and kissed her nose before he stood. "Why don't you call Deidre and check on the cat—did you name her? —while I find my shoes?"

"Misty Kitty." Larissa slipped her phone from her pocket and opted to text instead. "I guess when I'm looking for a place, I need to remember I have a cat."

"She can stay here, if that's easier." Sean came back with a pair of sneakers in his hand. "She's our cat. Together."

LARISSA TOOK Mrs. Patterson's hand with a forced smile. The older woman was outspoken and caustic. And Matt's aunt. She tried to remember that. Matt was amazing and—from everything she'd gathered from Azure—Mrs. Patterson had done the bulk of raising him. She couldn't be all bad. But it felt like the woman could see straight into her soul.

"I'm so glad you made it today. Young people don't always value the importance of church on Sundays. Particularly when they're just passing through."

Larissa nodded. "Yes, ma'am. It's easy to get into vacation

mode and skip. But everyone at Peacock Hill speaks so highly of this church, I couldn't not come."

Mrs. Patterson seemed to wrestle with herself before she smiled. "You'll still be here for Matt and Azure's wedding?"

"I'll come back. But the private school in Richmond where I'm teaching starts August twenty-sixth and I have to report on the twelfth." Larissa paused and swallowed the little knot of panic that formed every time she thought about how close that was.

"That's two weeks." Mrs. Patterson angled her head. "Where will you be living?"

"I'm hoping to nail that down this week." She had to. The house rental thing wasn't happening. Not immediately. At this point, she'd be better off saving up for a down payment and buying. In the future. A far distant one. "I have a couple of possibilities and need to firm up a decision."

"So you're not moving in with that man—oh, you know the one? The handsome one helping Azure with the wedding."

"Sean. No, ma'am. That was never an option. Misty Kitty is, though. He's home more during the day, so it seemed more fair for her to live with him."

Mrs. Patterson nodded. "Well. I'll be praying for you to find the right place. Matt says they're going to miss you at Peacock Hill. I guess you've become good friends with Azure?"

Larissa nodded. That had been a bit of a surprise. Azure was different from anyone Larissa had ever known. "She's an amazing woman. Matt's lucky to have her."

"Blessed, dear. Luck isn't something Christians rely on."

It was a figure of speech. Larissa fought the eye roll and smiled instead. "Of course. It's what I meant."

"Aunt Ida." Matt slid his arm around his aunt's shoulders. "Uncle Jim's been looking for you. Some of the ladies are trying to organize an end-of-summer potluck and you know they can't do that without you."

"Oh, my. In the fellowship hall?"

Matt nodded.

"It was so nice to see you, dear." Mrs. Patterson patted Larissa's arm before dashing toward the stairs.

"Thank you."

Matt laughed. "Sorry it took me so long to get over here. You ready to head up? Deidre said you caught a ride down, but she had to leave early."

That explained why Larissa hadn't been able to find Deidre in the lingering crowd. "Yeah. Thanks."

"Sean coming down this afternoon?" Matt led her across the parking lot to Azure's old truck. Azure was already inside.

With a grin, Azure scooted to the middle of the bench seat. "Hey."

"Hey, yourself. And yes, that's the plan." Larissa hoisted herself up onto the passenger seat.

"What plan?" Azure's glance traveled between Matt and Larissa.

"Sean coming down this afternoon. He said he had news, but wouldn't tell me over the phone." Larissa sighed. "Who knew the man loved surprises?"

"Doesn't everyone?"

"No, Azure. Not everyone loves surprises." Especially not when so much of her life was already up in the air. Having something else sprung on her was the opposite of what Larissa wanted right now. But no amount of wheedling had worked to get Sean to spill the beans.

"Ah, well. He'll be here soon. Who's on lunch today?" Azure looked over at Matt. "It wasn't us, right?"

"It was. But since I agreed to give Larissa a ride home, Deidre agreed to grab a couple of buckets of chicken on her way back up to the house. It seemed like a good trade."

"That works. You're staying for lunch, right?"

Larissa nodded. She'd tried to get out of it once already. Since the probability was high that she'd be moving back to Richmond this week, Deidre had put her foot down. Claire had backed her sister up. Larissa hadn't argued. In the spring, she'd resented their attempts to make her part of the Peacock Hill gang. Now? She was grateful they'd been persistent. It was good to have more friends—people who would be around no matter what.

Sean's car was already parked by the stand of cedars in front of the house when they arrived. Larissa hopped down from the truck and hurried toward the house. Matt and Azure's laughter followed her, but she didn't care. She hadn't seen Sean since she'd been in Richmond on Tuesday. Phone calls—even video calls—weren't the same.

He stood on the landing of the stairs under the enormous stained glass window, holding the cat. Larissa's heart seemed to stop for a moment before taking off again double-time. She hurried up the stairs to meet him.

"Hi. You're early."

Sean set the cat down before pulling Larissa close. "I went to the early service. I was up—thinking of you and anxious to be here—so I figured I might as well."

"I'm so glad." Larissa wound her arms around him and laid her head on his shoulder. "I missed you. It seems ridiculous, but—"

"It seems normal. I love you." Sean kissed her forehead.

The main door opened, and Matt and Azure strolled in.

"Told you." Azure laughed. "Since you're here, I have a couple of wedding thoughts. When you have a minute. Is that okay?"

"Sure." Sean angled his head to meet Larissa's gaze. "Is it okay if we talk shop for a little?"

"Of course. But first you need to tell me the surprise. For the record? I hate surprises."

Sean chuckled. "Noted. It's good news, I think. I mentioned your apartment hunt to the front office of my complex. They called me last night and said they had a unit opening up. A tenant breaking their lease. It's just one bedroom, so they don't have a waiting list. If you want it, you can move in as early as Friday. Otherwise they'll list it."

Larissa blinked. She'd been thinking two bedrooms, because that's what she'd had before. But she'd been fine in the studio in Brazil. It wasn't a terrible idea to downsize some of her stuff anyway. Not if she'd be merging her life with Sean's in the next year. Wait. The next year? She pushed that away. They could talk timing later. Maybe sign up for premarital counseling and see if the pastor had insight on that. "I want it."

"I hoped you would. It's a building over, but that's what? A three-minute walk?

Larissa looked away and saw Misty Kitty sitting regally near the base of the steps. "I can visit the cat whenever I want."

"The cat?" Sean pretended offense, but his eyes danced. "Just the cat?"

"Is there someone else I need to visit?" She laughed as his fingers drilled into her ribs. "Okay, okay. And you. I can see you whenever I want."

"And?"

"And that seems just about perfect." Larissa took a breath and started to ease back. "Go and help Matt and Azure. Their wedding is what, a month away?"

Sean nodded. "About that, yeah. Getting down to the wire."

"Then they can have you help them plan their future now, because we have all the time we need to plan our life together."

Larissa looked up and held his gaze for a heartbeat before easing up on her toes and joining her mouth to his.

"Our life together. I like the sound of that," Sean murmured against her mouth.

Larissa's lips curved under his kiss and she sent up a short, grateful prayer that her heart had been redirected from the path she'd chosen to the one God set out.

Thank you so much for reading A Heart Redirected! I loved having the chance to explore life as a wedding planner with Sean (fun fact: I used to do some wedding planning for the church where I was a secretary. It's a lot of fun. And stress. And ultimately a little to extroverted for me.)

I can't wait for you to spend more time with Topher and Vanessa in the next book. That's right — giggling, flirty Vanessa and Topher, the baker who can't stand her. As much as I adore friends-to-more stories, I'm excited about this enemies-to-more tale, too.

I see a lot of drama in their future - won't you come along for the ride?

To be the first to know about Topher and Vanessa's story, A Heart Rearranged, you'll want to make sure you're signed up for my newsletter. You can do that here: www.ElizabethMaddrey.com/monthly-newsletter-sign-up

SNEAK PEEK OF A HEART REARRANGED, PEACOCK HILL BOOK 5

"Why are you in here?"

Vanessa Fisher turned, scowling, and saw Topher Adams standing next to three large, rolling coolers with his arms crossed. The guy might be hot, but he defined unfriendly and hard to work with. "Checking on the flowers in here. Which I see you moved. Again."

"They were in my way. I'll put them back when I'm finished setting up. You should know better than to dress the cake area before the cake is in place."

"Seems to me I got the same schedule you did. I just happened to stick to it."

Red flooded Topher's face and neck. His jaw twitched and he spoke through gritted teeth. "I kept Sean informed of the delay."

"Well he didn't say anything to me." Vanessa crossed her arms and held his stare. If he thought he was going to intimidate her, he had another think coming. The wedding planner should have kept her in the loop. She'd take that up with Sean later.

"And I believe Sean has talked to you about moving my flowers. Several times."

"They were in the way."

"They wouldn't have been if you'd been on time!" Vanessa took a deep breath and tried to focus over the blood thundering in her ears. She was not going to get into another shouting match with him. No matter how annoying and obnoxious he was.

"Whatever. I'll let you know when you can put stuff back. I'd planned to do it, it's not like it's hard."

She clamped her teeth together. She was not going to respond. Was. Not. Going. To. Huffing out a breath that was closer to a strangled scream, Vanessa spun on her heel and stomped from the climate-controlled tent into a wall of wet summer heat that exemplified Virginia in September.

Sean jogged toward her, winding through the tables set up in front of the lion-head fountain, whose sprawling pool stretched the entire width of the area behind Peacock Hill. "Vanessa!"

She crossed her arms and waited.

"Hey. Topher's a little behind schedule."

"I know that now." She glanced over her shoulder at the tent then frowned at Sean. "He moved my flowers."

Sean winced. "Sorry. I meant to let you know to shuffle the dessert tent to last. Did he say when he'd be finished setting things up?"

"Of course not, that would've been helpful. But after you find out, can you let me know?" She'd go double-check the flower setup in the foyer where the ceremony would take place. Maybe by the time she finished that, she could fix the flowers in the tent. She sure wasn't going to let Topher put things back.

Sean sighed and tucked his hands in his pockets. "Come on. Can't we all be adults?"

"I am not the one being childish here. That—he—argh!" She

broke off as Sean strode into the tent. Fine. She followed him back into the cool tent. Let Topher explain his behavior with an audience. Of course, Topher and Sean were friends, so she'd probably still end up on the losing end.

"—that's why I called and said I was running behind. It's not my fault she put flowers in here before the cake was set. Seriously, who does that?"

"Someone trying to stick to the schedule she was given." Vanessa jumped in before Sean could speak.

Sean held up his hands. "Look, this is on me, okay? I get that. It's my bad. Vanessa, why don't you give Topher your cell number? Then he can text you when he's done in here and you don't have to wait for him to tell me and then for me to have time to let you know. Azure and the attendants are going to need their flowers soon. The foyer and staircase already looks amazing, so I know you'll have time to get the tent finished before it becomes an issue."

"I can put everything back. I took pictures before I moved things." Topher waggled his cell phone. "It's not like it's hard."

"You will not touch the flowers again." Vanessa fought the urge to glare at Topher. She had to maintain some semblance of professionalism in front of Sean if she wanted him to keep sending business her way. She liked coming out to Peacock Hill. Sure, it was a bit of a hike from Richmond, but the venue was amazing. There were so many possible locations for a ceremony and reception. She'd been elated when Azure said the ceremony itself would be inside. Too bad the reception was out in the Labor Day swelter.

"Topher." Sean shot a firm glance toward the caterer. "He'll text you when he's set, right?"

"Fine." Topher held out his phone. "Put your number in. I'll label it later."

She could only imagine the name he'd choose. Two could

play that game. Vanessa tapped in her number and handed the phone back. "I'll wait for your text. I should get up to the bride."

Topher rolled his eyes.

Vanessa narrowed her gaze and poked her finger into his chest. "Don't. Touch. The. Flowers."

Irritating, annoying, obnoxious, interfering, insulting, aggravating man.

That was the only reason he made her pulse race.

It had nothing to do with his sea green eyes and broad shoulders.

Not. One. Thing.

ACKNOWLEDGMENTS

I'd be remiss if I didn't take a few minutes to thank the people who make writing possible. First (always and forever), I'm thankful to Jesus for putting stories in my head and giving me words when I sit down to write. I couldn't do any of this without Him and it is my tiny little act of worship.

Thanks also go to my husband and kids for giving me space to write. Sometimes this means dinner is quesadillas, again, because I got caught up with people who are only real on paper. I'm grateful we all still love melty cheese. Thanks for your patience and belief (and for thinking it's kind of cool that mom writes books. I think it's kind of cool, too.)

To my writer friends - in particular Valerie Comer, Heather Gray, and Lynnette Bonner. Thanks for taking time out of your own busy lives to read and give feedback on the story. For encouraging me and letting me whine and reminding me that we can only write the stories God puts on our hearts. Even when they're a little scary.

I didn't set out to write a book that touched on homosexuality and the Christian. In fact, this book took a long time to write primarily, I think, because I was struggling a la Jonah hopping on a ship in the opposite direction with going there in even the smallest manner. But it's a part of our life today and I think it's critical that Christians not shy away from engaging with the culture in a loving, Jesus-honoring way. To me, the first step in this process is to remember that we are all sinners. Every single one of us. The only difference between me, as a believer in Jesus, and anyone else is that I am saved by grace through faith. It's my dearest prayer that we would all seek to live in that grace and share it with those around us and help them see that it is possible to turn from sin and live a new life in Christ.

Finally, I want each and every person who picks up one of my books to know that I appreciate you. There are so many worthwhile books in the marketplace today. I'm honored that you chose to spend your time and hard-earned money on mine.

ALSO BY ELIZABETH MADDREY

Hope Ranch Series

Hope for Christmas

Peacock Hill Romance Series

A Heart Restored

A Heart Reclaimed

A Heart Realigned

Arcadia Valley Romance – Baxter Family Bakery Series

Loaves & Wishes

Muffins & Moonbeams

Cookies & Candlelight

Donuts & Daydreams

The 'Operation Romance' Series

Operation Mistletoe

Operation Valentine

Operation Fireworks

Operation Back-to-School

The 'Taste of Romance' Series

A Splash of Substance

A Pinch of Promise

A Dash of Daring

A Handful of Hope

A Tidbit of Trust

The 'Grant Us Grace' Series

Joint Venture

Wisdom to Know

Courage to Change

Serenity to Accept

Pathway to Peace

The 'Remnants' Series:

Faith Departed

Hope Deferred

Love Defined

Stand alone novellas

Kinsale Kisses: An Irish Romance

Luna Rosa (part of A Tuscan Legacy)

Non-Fiction

A Walk in the Valley: Christian encouragement for your journey through infertility

For the most recent listing of all my books, please visit my website.

ABOUT THE AUTHOR

Elizabeth Maddrey is a semi-reformed computer geek and homeschooling mother of two who lives in the suburbs of Washington D.C. When she isn't writing, Elizabeth is a voracious consumer of books. She loves to write about Christians who struggle through their lives, dealing with sin and receiving God's grace on their way to their own romantic happily ever after.

facebook.com/ElizabethMaddrey

instagram.com/ElizabethMaddrey

amazon.com/author/elizabethmaddrey

bookbub.com/authors/elizabeth-maddrey

www.ingramcontent.com/pod-product-compliance
Lightning Source LLC
Chambersburg PA
CBHW020907180626
46816CB00007BA/2280